John Stephen Farmer

National Ballad and Song

Merry Songs and Ballads, Prior to the Year A.D. 1800

John Stephen Farmer

National Ballad and Song
Merry Songs and Ballads, Prior to the Year A.D. 1800

ISBN/EAN: 9783744777957

Printed in Europe, USA, Canada, Australia, Japan

Cover: Foto ©Andreas Hilbeck / pixelio.de

NATIONAL BALLAD AND SONG

Merry Songs and Ballads

PRIOR TO THE YEAR A.D. 1800

EDITED BY

JOHN S. FARMER

VOLUME V

PRIVATELY PRINTED FOR SUBSCRIBERS ONLY

MDCCCXCVII

INDEX

TO VOL. V

AUTHORS, TITLES, FIRST LINES, REFRAINS, AND SOURCES

Merry Songs and Ballads

THE BRIDE'S FIRST NIGHT

[*c.* 1610-20]

[By "W. C."; from *Rawlinson MS.*, Poet. 214, leaf 71, back].

Being entered, and the bed with all thinges sett,
Vpon the side thereof a while they sitt.
when left alone, they talke and toy & smile,
She, whilst she canne, the tyme seeks to beguile,
till sudingly her cheekes are all bewept,
to loose so soone what she so long hath kept;
& oft she castes her eyes vpon the place
where she is to wrastle; and she highdes her face.
He with such gentle force compells the Lasse,
as would not breake her, were she made of glasse,
so loth he is to hurt her; yet he throwghs
her softly downe, and to her side he growes.
Venus begins to teach them a new trade,
The marrage quene here playes the chamber-maide:
Juno her-selfe, whose new affections growne,
and there attends to teach them Marse vnknowne,

the whilst he seekes for babyes in her eyes,
feeles her white neck, & ivery breasts that rise
Like 2 white snowy hills, and still doth praise
all that he feeles or touches; then thus sayes:
"O frish and flourishing Virgin now in brid,
and are you growne at length so near my side;
of all my hopes the storehouse and the treasure,
my long-expected, now my greatest pleasure;
my sweet & dearest loue, this could not be
nor happen thus, but by the gods decree;
& will [you] now the power of loue withstande?"
at this she turnes, & stayes his forward hand,
trembling to think of that which was to ensue,
or proue the thinge which yet she neuer knew;
twixt hope and fear she thus replyes:
"O faire and louely youth, list t' a Virgins prayre!
of the ingrate, by those which gaue the such,
thy parents bee, I only beg thus much:
pitty my tears, put me to noe affright,
I only craue repriue but for this night"
with [that] she seemes intraunst, and prostrate lyes,
hath not one word to vtter more, nor eyes
to see herselfe vnvirgeyned, winkes, lyes still,
& since be needes must, letts him act his will:
betwixt them too, they quench loues amorrous fires,
she what she feares, he what he long desires.

THE NEW EXCHANGE

[1610-20]

[From *Rawlinson MS.*, Poet. B 35, leaf 44; another version in *Wit Restored*, p. 138].

Ile go no more to the old Exchange,
  There's no good ware at all;
There bodkins are, and thimbles to,
  Long since sent to Geldhall;
But we will go to the new Exchange,
  Where are all things in fashion,
And henceforth we will have it called,
  The bush of reformation.
    Come lords and ladyes,
    And se what you lack:
    Here are all sorts of prizes:
    Here's long and short: here's wide and straight:
    Here are all sorts of sizes.

Madam, if you please you may fit yourselfe
  With all good sorts of pins;
Se, here is fur, & here is hayre;
  Here's gold & cornelean rings;

And for to keep your fingers warme,
 Here's Bossell & sable muffs.
  Come lords and ladyes, &c.

Maddam, if you please, Ile shew you good sport
 For crouding, neere fear that,
Against a stall, or upon a stoole,
 Your selfe for to recreate:
Here's childrens bables, and mens tooles,
 To play with for delight,
And here's round heads when they turn euery way
 At length will stand upright.
  Come lords and ladyes, &c.

Here's dice and boxes, if you please
 To play at in and in;
Here's brows for horns, and horns for brows
 That never will be seene.
Here is a set of kitle pins,
 & boules at them to roule;
& if you like such thundering spourt,
 Here is my ladys hole.
  Come lords and ladyes, &c.

Here's shaddows setting of all sorts
 As various as your minds;
Here is a windmill like your selfe,
 Will turne at every wind;
Here's a church of the same stuff,

Cut out in the new fashion;
Here is a priest stands twice a day,
Will please your congregation.
Come lords and ladyes, &c.

Here patches are of every cut,
For pimples and for scars:
Here are the wandring plannets & signes,
The moon & fixed stars,
All ready gumm'd to make them stick:
You need no other sky
Nor star for Lilly for to view,
To tell your fortunes by.
Come lords and ladyes, &c.

Here's perewigs will fitt all heads,
False beards for a disguise,
Will help all maidens that are bare
In all parts of their thighes,
If you enjoy well, here you may
Take up fine holland smoks,
Which have all things that women ware,
Except Italian locks.
Come lords and ladyes, &c.

Here are your boys, with backs like bulls,
At first sight can leap lasses,
And some there are, hold out like gulls,
And some there be, like asses,

Here are you[r] gallants can out do,
Your vsshers or your pages;
You need not go to Ludgate more,
till 3 score years of age.
Come lords and ladyes, &c.

Come lords and ladyes, se what you lack;
Here is ware of all prizes;
Here's long and short, here's wide, here's straight,
And seven all sorts of sizes.
Come lords and ladyes,
And se what you lack:
Here are all sorts of prizes:
Here's long and short: here's wide and straight:
Here are all sorts of sizes.

"WHY DO YOU TRIFLE? FY UPON'T!"

[*c.* 1610-20]

[From *Rawlinson MS.*, B 35, leaf 54, back].

Why do you trifle? fy upon't, fie upon't, fie upon't,
    fy upon't!
Why do you trifle? fy upon't!
Those are not men but idle drones,
That stay till ladyes make their mones;
tis pity but they lost their [stones];
fy upon't, fy upon't, fy upon't!
Tis pity but they lost their labour.

He shall not do so that I love, that I love, that
    I love,
He shall not do so that I love;
But so soone as I am sick,
Shall never faile me in the nick,
To give me proof of his good [prick]
That I love, that I love, that I love,
To give me proofe of his good meaning.

Nor can it be to thick and long, thick and long, thick
    and long,

If any of you chance to feare
That I am to young,—pray look you here;
Few maids can show you so much [haire]
Thick and long, thick and long, thick and long,
Few maids can shew you so much faivour.

Faine would I goe both up and downe, up and
downe, up and downe,
No child is fonder of the Gig
Than I to dance a merry jig;
Faine would I try how I could [fig]
Up and downe, up and downe, up and downe,
Faine would I try how I could caper.

Come let us do then, you know what, you know
what, you know what,
Why should not I endure the brunt
As well as other maids have don't?
I'm sure I have as good a [cunt],
You know what, you know what, you know what,
[I'm sure I] have as good a courage.

Sweet, if you love me then agen, then agen, then
agen,
Had ever maiden that good luck
For to incounter the first pluck?
O 'twould invite a maid to [fuck]
Then agen, then agen, then agen,
O 'twould invite a maid to mary.

A DALLING WITH A LADY

[*c.* 1610-20]

[By "Mr. Mark P."; from *Rawlinson MS.*, Poet. 214, leaf 75, back].

Nay pish, nay fy, nay out afont!
for shame! nay, take away your hand!
in faith, you are to blame.
nay come, this fooling must not bee;
nay pish, nay fy; you tickle mee.

Your buttons scrub me, you crumple my band,
You hurt my thighs; pray take away your hand;
the dore stands open, that all may see;
nay pish, nay fy; you tickle mee.

When you and I shall mett in place,
both togeather, face to face,
Ile not cry out; then you, then you shall see:
nay pish, nay fi; you tickle mee.

But now I see my wordes are but vaine,
for I haue done't, why should I complane?
the way is open, & all is free;
since tis noe more, pray tickle mee.

O WATT! WHERE ART THO

[*c.* 1620-50]

[From *Percy Folio MSS.*].

Iff mourne I may in tyme soe glad,
or mingle ioyes *w*ith dytty sadd,
lend me *you*r eares, lend watt *you*r eyes,
& see you where shee tombed lyyes.
too simple ffoote, alas, containes
the Lasse *tha*t Late on downes & plaines
made horsse & hound & horne to blowe.
O watt! where art thou? who, ho, ho!

O where is now thy fflight so ffleete,
thy iealous brow & ffearffull ffeete,
thy suttle traine & courses stronge,
thy capers hye & dances Longe?
who sees thee now in couert creepe,
to stand & harke, or sitt & weepe,
to Coole thy ffeet, to ffoyle thy ffoe?
O watt! where art thou? who, ho, ho!

where is thy vew & sweating sent
*tha*t soe much blood & breath hath spent?

thy magicke ffriske & cirkelles round,
thy iugling ffeates to mocke the hound?
why didst thou not, this doome to scape,
vpon thee take some witches shape,
& shrowd thy selfe in cottage Lowe?
O watt! where art thou? who, ho, ho!

But why shold wee thinke watt soe wise
as Ioulers noyse, or Iumbells cryes,
or Ladyes Lipps? on watt alone
must needs by many be ore-throwen.
but as I moane thy liffe soe short,
soe will I sing thy royall sport,
& guiltelesse gaine of all I know.
O watt! where art thou? who, ho, ho!

why didst thou not then ffly this ffate?
ffrom fforth her fforme put fforth thy make?
as some good wiffe, when deathes att doore,
will put her goodman fforth before.
thy enuious leaues, & thy muse,
as p*er*ffect once as maidens scuse;
thy tracke in snow, like widowes woe.
O watt! where art thou? who, ho, ho!

Once cold thou strangly see behind;
now art thou round about thee blyind.
both Male & ffemale once wert thou;
O neither Male nor ffemall now!

thy hermitts liffe, thy dreadffull crosse,
thy sweating striffe & clickett close,
when once thou wert both Bucke and doe.
O watt! where art thou? who, ho, ho!

O, had the ffaire young sonne of Mirrh
fforsooke the bore, & ffollow[ed] her;
or had Acteon hunted watt
when he saw Cynthias you know whatt;
or *th*at young man knowne *th*at liffe
*th*at slew ffor deere his deares[t] wiffe,
they all had knowne no other woe,
but watt! where art thou? who, ho, ho!

Shrill sounding hornes & siluer bells
shall sound thy mortts, & ring thy knell:
young shepards shall thy storry tell,
& bonny Nimphes sing thy ffarwell,
& hunters alltogether Ioyne
to drowned both woe and watt in wine,
whiles I conclude my song euen soe;
O watt! where art thou? who, ho, ho!

"MY MISTRESS IS A LADY"

[*c.* 1649-60]

[By T. PRESWICK; from *Rawlinson MS.*, Poet. 214, leaf 75, back].

My Mistres is a Lady
& shes a fine as may be;
She is as fine as the muses 9,
or any bartholomew baby.

Her buttock is a round one,
& her Ct perfumed too;
her lips are as red as radle,
& she hath more haire vpon her ware
than will stufe a troopers sadle.

God blesse my Lord protector,
& allso his protectoures;
Let all men live in feare of him
and euery man loue his Mistres.

My Mistres is a woman,
& her Ct is grown so common;
have a care of your tarse,

Least she fire it with her arse,
for she is free for all men.

Her eyes are as bright
as the starres of the light;
oh, how they doe twenckle!
if she had a thousand pound,
she would throught on the ground,
for the love of a standing pinckle.

THE MERRY BAG-PIPES:

THE PLEASANT PASTIME BETWIXT A JOLLY SHEPHERD AND A COUNTRY DAMSEL, ON A MID-SUMMERS-DAY IN THE MORNING

[*c.* 1650]

[From *Roxburgh Ballads*, ii. 236; tune, *March boys, &c.*; music in *Pills to Purge Melancholy* (1707), iii. 136].

A Shepherd set him under a Thorn,
he pull'd out his Pipe and began for to play,
It was on a *Mid-summers-day* in the morn,
for honour of that Holy-day:
A Ditty he did Chant along,
goes to the Tune of *Cater-Bordee*
And this was the burthen of his Song,
if thou wilt Pipe Lad, I'll dance to thee,
To thee, to thee, derry, derry, to thee, &c.

And whilst this Harmony he did make,
a Country Damsel from the Town,
A Basket on her Arm she had,
a gathering Rushes on the Down;

Her Bongrace of wended Straw;
  from the Sun's hot Beams her Face is free,
And thus she began when she him saw,
  if thou wilt Pipe Lad, I'll dance to thee,
    To thee, to thee, derry, derry, to thee, &c.

Then he pull'd out his Pipe, and began to sound,
  whilst tempting on her Back she lay,
But when his quivering note she found,
  how sweetly then this Lass could play:
She stop'd all jumps, and she reveal'd,
  she kept all time with harmony,
And looking on him, sighing said,
  if thou wilt Pipe Lad, I'll Dance to thee,
    To thee, to thee, derry, derry, to thee, &c.

She never so much as blusht at all,
  the Musick was so charming sweet,
But e'er anon to him she'd call,
  and bid him be active, turn and meet;
As thou art a bonny Shepherd's Swain,
  I am a Lass am come to Wooe thee,
To play me another double Strain,
  and doubt not but I will Dance to thee,
    To thee, to thee, derry, derry, to thee, &c.

Altho' I am but a silly Maid,
  who ne'er was brought up at Dancing-School,
But yet to the Jig that thou hast plaid,

you find that I can keep time and Rule:
Now see that you keep your stops aright,
for Shepherd, I am resolv'd to view thee,
And play me the Damsel's chief Delight,
then never doubt but I'll Dance to thee,
To thee, to thee, derry, derry, to thee, &c.

The Shepherd again did Tune his Pipe,
and plaid her a Lesson loud and shrill,
The Damsel his Face did often wipe,
with many a Thank for his good will;
And said, I was ne'er so pleas'd before,
and this is the first time that I knew thee,
Come play me this very Jigg once more,
and never doubt but I'll Dance to thee,
To thee, to thee, derry, derry, to thee, &c.

The Shepherd, he said, as I am a Man,
I have kept Playing from Morning till Noon,
Thou know'st I can do no more than I can;
my Pipe is clearly out of Tune;
To ruine a Shepherd I'll not seek,
said she, for why should I undo thee,
I can come again to the Down next Week,
and thou shalt Pipe, and I'll Dance to thee,
To thee, to thee, derry, derry, to thee, &c.

"AS I TRAVERS'D TO AND FRO"

[*c.* 1650]

[From the *Academy of Compliments*, p. 199].

As I travers'd to and fro,
And in the fields was walking,
I chanc'd to hear two Sisters
  That secretly were talking:
The younger to the elder said,
Prethee why do'st not marry?
  In faith, quoth she, I'le tell to thee,
  I mean not long to tarry.

When I was fifteen years of age,
Then I had suitors many:
But, I a wanton peevish wench
Would not sport with any:
Till at the last I sleeping fast,
Cupid came to woo me,
And, like a lad that was stark mad,
He swore he would come to me.

And then he lay down by my side
And spread his armes upon me,
And I, being 'twixt sleep and wake,
Did strive to thrust him from me,
But he with all the power he had,
Did lie the harder on me.
And then he did so play with me,
As I was plaid with never;
The wanton boy so pleased me,
I would have slept for ever.
And then methought the world turn'd round,
And *Phœbus* fell a-skipping,
And all the Nymphs and Goddesses
About us two were tripping.
Then seemed *Neptune* as he had pour'd
His Ocean streams upon us,
But *Boreas* with his blust'ring blasts
Did strive to keep him from us.
Limping *Vulcan* he came,
As if he had been jealous,
Venus follow'd after him,
And swore she'd blow the bellows.
Mars called *Cupid* Jackanapes,
And swore he would him smother,
Quoth *Cupid*, Said I so to thee
When thou lay'st with my mother?
Juno then, and *Jupiter*,
Came marching with *Apollo*;

Pan came in with *Mercury*,
And then began the hollo;
Cupid ran and hid himself,
And so of joys bereft me:
For suddenly I did awake,
And all these fancies left me.

AN HISTORICAL BALLAD

[*c.* 1660]

[From *Ane Pleasant Garden* (*c.* 1800); supposed to refer to Lady Southesk, mistress of the Duke of York, afterwards James II].

Much has been said of strumpets of yore,
Of Lais whole volumes, of Messaline more,
But I sing of a lewder than e'er lived before
Which nobody can deny.

From her mother at first shee drew the infection,
And as soon as shee spoke, she made use of injection,
And now shee's grown up to a girl of perfection,
Which nobody can deny.

If you told her of hell, she would say't was a jest,
And swear of all gods, that Priapus was best,
For her soul was a whore, when she suck't at ye breast,
Which her nurses can't deny.

She once was call'd virgin, but t'was but a shamm,
Her maidenhead never was gotten by man,

She frigg'd it away in the womb of her damm,
Which the midwife couldn't deny.

At length Mr. Foppling made her his bride,
But found (to bring down his ambition and pride)
Her fortune but narrow, and her c—t very wide,
Which he himself can't deny.

In vain he long strove to satiate her lust,
Which still grew more vig'rous at every thrust,
No wonder the puny chitt came by the worst,
Which nobody can deny.

For when hee grew sapless, shee gave him her blessing,
And left him to painting, to patching, and dressing,
But first dubb'd him cuckold, a strange way of jesting,
Which nobody can deny.

And now shee is free to swive where she pleases,
And where e're she swives, she scatters diseases,
And a shanker's a damn'd loveing thing where it seizes,
Which nobody can deny.

There's Haughton, and Elland, and Arran the sott,
(Shee deserves to be pox'd that would f—k with a Scott,)

All charged the lewd harlott, and all went to pott,
Which they themselves can't deny.

For that shee has bubo'd and ruin'd as many
As Hinton, or Willis, Moll Howard, or any,
And, like to those punks, will f—k for a penny,
Is what nobody can deny.

To scower the town is her darling delight,
In breaking of windows, to scratch, and to fight,
And to ly with her own brawny footman at night,
Which she herself can't deny.

Who, though they eternally pizzle her britch,
Can't allay the wild rage of her letch'rous itch,
Which proves our good lady a monstrous bitch,
Which they themselves can't deny.

But now if there's any, or Christian, or Jew,
That say I've bely'd her, I advise 'em to goe
And ask the fair creature herself if 't is true,
Which I'm certain shee won't deny.

CONTENTMENT

[1661]

[From *Merry Drollerie*, p. 161].

What though the Times produce effects
  Are worth our observation,
He's mad that at it once dejects,
  Or does remove his station;
Give me the Wench, that's like a Tench
  In holding up her belly
For to receive, and to conceive
  The most heroick Jelly.

Although she be a Saint that's free
  From any such intention,
She may be bold, hang her that's cold,
  With a timerous apprehension:
Let danger come have at her Bum,
  Give me the Girle that stands to't,
And when it's lanck, does advance her Flank
  And lay a helping hand to't.

To make it rise between her thighs
  And firk her is a pleasure;

Tho he be stout he ne'er comes out,
  But he wants of his measure:
If he have a yard it will be hard
  If he half a one produces;
When he's so short you may thank her for't,
  Oh these are gross abuses.

My Mistris she is very free,
  And fancies well my temper:
Sweet Rogue, she loves the merry shoves,
  And is clear from all distemper;
When I stand to it, she needs must do it,
  For she is compos'd of pleasure,
And does invite me to delight,
  I exhaust my chiefest treasure.

My Mistris she is very free,
  And sings and frolicks neatly:
Besides all this, she does nobly kiss
  And does her work compleatly,
For which I love her, and none above her,
  And she loves me for the same too;
But that I fear you'ld soon be there,
  I would disclose her name too.

LOVES TENEMENT

[1661]

[From *Merry Drollery*, pt. ii. p. 64; *cf.* "A tenement to let," *Merry Songs*, iv.].

If any one do want a house
Prince, Duke, Earl, Lord, or Squire,
Or Peasant, hardly worth a louse,
I can fit his desire:
I have a Tenement, the which
I know can fit them all,
'Tis seated near a stinking ditch,
Men call it Cony-hall.

It stands below Bum Alley,
A foot of belly hill;
This Tenement is to be ta'n
By whosoever will;
For term of years, for months, or daies,
I'll let this pleasant bower,
Nay, rather than a Tenant want,
I'll let it for an houre.

About it grows a pleasant wood
To shade you from the Sun;

Well watered 'tis, for through the house
A pleasant stream doth run;
If hot, you there may cool you,
If cold, you there find heat,
For little it not greatest is,
For least 'tis not too great.

My house, indeed, I must say is dark,
Be it by night or day,
But if that you be gotten in
You cannot miss the way;
None ever yet within my house
Did ever weep or wail,
You need not fear the tenure of it,
For it is held in tayle.

But I must covenant with him
That takes this house of mine,
Hither for years, or else for months,
Or for some shorter time,
That once a day he wash it,
And sweep it round about
And if that he do fail of this
I'll seek a new Tenant out.

Thus if you like my Tenement,
Your house room shall be good,
Of such a temper as you shall
Need burn neither Cole or wood;

For be it cold or be it hot,
To speak I dare be bold,
As long as you keep your nose within dores
You never shall be a cold.

MINE OWN SWEET HONEY-BIRD-CHUCK

[1661]

[From *Merry Drollerie*, p. 155].

Mine own sweet honey-bird-chuck
  Come sit thee down by me,
And thou and I will truck
  For thy Commodity:
The Weather is cold and chilly,
  And heating will do thee no harm,
I'll put a hot thing in thy belly
  To keep thy body warm.

Our Landlady hath brought us
  All that the house affords,
'Tis time to lay about us,
  Then prethee make no words:
I know thou art young and tender,
  Although thy cunt be rough,
Thy Fort if thou'lt to me surrender,
  I'll man it well enough.

I find by thy whispering Palm-sweat,
  And thine eyes like noon,

Thy panting breasts, as thy pulse, beat,
  Thou'lt do it to some tune;
Then give thy mind to it, my honny,
  Thou shalt never have cause to rue,
That ever thou hazard'st thy Cunny
  To one of the jovial Crew.

"FULL FORTY TIMES OVER"

[1661]

[From *Merry Drollery*, p. 61].

Full forty times over I have strived to win,
Full forty times over repulsed have been,
But 'tis forty to one but I'll tempt her agen:
For he's a dull Lover
That so will give over,
Since thus runs the sport,
Since thus runs the sport,
Assault her but often, and you carry the Fort,
Since thus runs the sport,
Assault her but often, and you carry the Fort.

Theres a breach ready made, which still open hath
been,
With thousand of thoughts to betray it within,
If you once but approach you are sure to get in,
Then stand not off coldly,
But venter on boldly,
With weapon in hand,
With weapon in hand,

If you once but approach, she's not able to stand,
With weapon in hand:
If you once but approach, she's not able to stand.

Some Lady-birds when down before them you sit,
Will think to repulse you with Fire-balls of wit,
But alas they'r but crackers, and seldome do hit;
Then vanquish them after
With alarms of laughter,
Their Forces being broke,
Their Forces being broke,
And the fire quite out, you may vanquish in smoak:
Their Forces being broke,
And the fire quite out, you may vanquish in smoak.

With pride & with state, some out-works they make,
And with Volleys of frowns drive the enemy back:
If you mind her discreetly she's easie to take,
Then to it, ne'r fear her,
But boldly come near her,
By working about,
By working about:
If you once but approach, she can ne'r hold it out,
By working about,
If you once but approach, she can ne'r hold it out.

Some Ladies with blushes and modesty fight,
And with their own fears the rude foe do affright,

But they'r eas'ly surpriz'd if you come in the night;
Then this you must drive at,
To parley in private,
And then they're o'rthrown,
And then they're o'rthrown,
If you promise them farely, they'l soon be your own,
And then they're o'rthrown,
If you promise them farely, they'l soon be your own.

THE SOULDIER

[1661]

[From *Merry Drollery*, p. 168].

Hey ho! have at all,
Fair Lady by your leave,
He that chanceth low to fall,
The higher must he heave;
Nay, faith, good Sir, you are too blame,
'Tis fashion for a clown,
For he that mounts too high at first,
Is soonest taken down.

I am a Souldier, bonny Lass,
And oft have fought in field,
In Battels oft as fierce as *Mars*,
Yet ne'er was forc'd to yield;
A Standard-bearer still am I,
And have broke many a Lance,
I have travell'd Countries far and nigh,
Yet ne'er was bound for *France*.

My Weapon it will stiffly stand,
And make a cunning thrust,

If I lye open to your hand,
So that you hit me just;
You are no cunning marks-man sure,
You lie so long at lure;
O thrust, thrust, thrust, far, far, far, far,
Be sure I will endure.

Fie, fie, your Lance doth bend,
Full little I account you,
Courageously if you'll not spend,
Sit fast, or I'll dismount you;
Such cowards fight I do disdain
That can endure no longer,
But see that when you come again
Your lance it may be stronger.

So so, now I see you have tricks by arts
Low, low, not so high,
You make my thighs to smart,
[*A line lost here*]
Your mounting high 'twill not be,
'Twill bring you soon to wrack,
I do not doubt the victory
Though I lie on my back.

A NEW YEAR'S GIFT

[1661]

[From *Merry Drollery*, p. 81].

Fair Lady for your New-year's gift
I send you here a dish of fruit:
The first shall be a Popering Pear,
'Tis all the fruit one tree doth bear;
Rowle it not, the juyce, I doubt,
'Tis so ripe, will all run out;
You must not pare it any whit,
But take it all in at one bit;
If in your mouth a while it lye,
It will melt deliciously.

The next in order doth befall,
Two handfull of great rouncefal;
King *Pryapus*, that Garden God,
Made *Venus* eat it in the Cod;
And since that seed all women sow,
Because it will so quickly grow;
If pretty Bun the stalk devour,
'Twil up again in half an hour;

When once the Bun it doth espy,
'Twill mop most prettily.

The next in order you shall have
A large Potato, and a brave:
It must be roasted in the fire
That *Cupid* kindled with desire,
The roasting it will mickle cost,
'Twill bast itself when it is roast,
It needs no sugar, nor no spice,
'Twill please a Stomack ne'r so nice;
'Twill make a maid at Midnight cry,
It comes most pleasantly.

The bravest thing in all this Land
You shall have *Mars* his holly wand:
A thing that never grew on tree,
'Twill t[o]uch and sting worse than a Bee;
Bend him not, perhaps in time
He may grow up unto his prime;
Correct him not too much at first,
For if you do, tears forth will burst;
When *Mars* came down to fetch his wand
It cries, I cannot stand.

A DREAM

[*c.* 1669]

[From PLAYFORD'S *Treasury of Musick*, ii. 28; music by HENRY LAWES].

I laid me down on a pillow soft,
And dream'd I clypt and kist my Mistress oft:
She cry'd, Fie, fie, away, you are too bold.
I pray'd her be content, tho' she were cold,
My veins did burn with flames of hot desire,
And must not leave till she had quench'd my
fire.
Well, since (said she) I may not from you fly,
Do what you please, I give you liberty.
With that I wak'd, but found I was deceiv'd;
For which I storm'd like one of sense bereav'd.

LOVES INGRATITUDE

[*c.* 1669]

[From PLAYFORD'S *Treasury of Musick*, i. 1; with music; set by Dr. WILSON].

Take, O take those *lips* away,
That so sweetly were forsworn,
And those *eys* that break of days,
Light that do mislead the morn,
But my kisses bring again,
Seals of love though seals in vain.

Hide, O hide those Hils of Snow
That thy frozen Blossome bears;
On whose tops the Pinks that grow,
Are yet of those that April wears:
But first set my poor heart free,
Bound in those Icy Chaines by thee.

THE WOOING ROGUE

[1671]

[From *Westminster Drollery*, pt. i. p. 16; tune, *My Freedom is all my Joy*].

Come live with me and be my Whore,
And we will beg from door to door
Then under a hedge we'l sit and louse us,
Until the Beadle come to rouse us
And if they'l give us no relief,
  Thou shalt turn Whore and I'l turn Thief.
  Thou shalt turn Whore and I'l turn Thief.

If thou canst rob, then I can steal,
And we'l eat Roast-meat every meal:
Nay, we'l eat white-bread every day
And throw our mouldy crusts away,
And twice a day we will be drunk,
  And then at night I'l kiss my Punk.
  And then at night I'l kiss my Punk.

And when we both shall have the Pox,
We then shall want both Shirts and Smocks,
To shift each others mangy hide,

That is with Itch so pockifi'd;
We'l take some clean ones from a hedge,
  And leave our old ones for a pledge.
  And leave our old ones for a pledge.

THE FAIRIES

[*c.* 1671]

[From *Bristol Drollery*, p. 61].

Come my *Jenny*, pretty one,
  Thee and I will all alone,
Hie to yonder Farie ground,
Where last night they trip'd around:
And (free from Mortal eyes) by stealth,
There skip'd and danc'd each little Elf.
  There, on the grass we'l sport and play,
  And thou shalt prove as light as they.
If *Corydon* and *Phillis* spie,
Or any bold intruding eye;
We'll pray transforming Gods above,
That we (like those) may Fairies prove.
And when we've changed shapes and hue,
We'll haunt, and fright, and pinch them too.

"MAKE READY, FAIR LADY, TO-NIGHT"

[1672]

[From *Windsor Drollery*, p. 231].

Make ready, fair Lady, to night;
Come down to the door below;
    For I will be there
    To receive you with care,
And with your true Love you shall go.

REPLY

And when the Stars twinkle so bright,
Then down to the door will I creep;
    To my Love I will fly,
    E'er the Jealous can spy,
And leave my old Dadde asleep.

"HAVE Y'ANY CRACKT MAIDENHEADS?"

[*c.* 1672]

[From *Windsor Drollery*, p. 162].

Have y'any crackt Maidenheads to new leach or
mend?
Have y'any old Maidenheads to sell or to change?
Bring 'em to me, with a little pretty gin,
I'll clout 'em, I'll mend 'em, I'll knock in a pin
Shall make 'em as good Maids agen
As ever they have been.

"I'D HAVE YOU, QUOTH HE"

[*c.* 1672]

[From *Windsor Drollery*, p. 157].

I'd have you, quoth he,
Wou'd you have me, quoth she,
O where, Sir.

In my Chamber, quoth he,
In your Chamber, quoth she,
Why there, Sir.

To kiss you, quoth he,
To kiss me, quoth she,
O why, Sir.

'Cause I love it, quoth he,
Do you love it, quoth she,
So do I, Sir.

"ALAS HOW LONG SHALL I AND MY MAIDENHEAD LIE"

[*c.* 1672]

[From *Windsor Drollery*, p. 39].

Alas how long shall I and my maidenhead lie:
In a cold bed all the night long!
I cannot abide it, yet away cannot chide it,
Though I find that it does me some wrong.

Can any one tell where this fine thing doth dwell,
That carries neither form nor fashion?
It both heats and cools, 'tis a Bauble for fools,
Yet catch'd at in every Nation.

Say a Maid were so crost, as to see this Toy lost,
Would not Hue and Cry fetch it again?
'Las no; for 'tis gon ere well thought upon;
And when found, 'tis lost even then.

"A WIFE I DO HATE"

[*c.* 1672]

[From *Windsor Drollery*, p. 14].

A Wife I do hate;
  For either she's false or she's jealous:
But give me a Mate
  That nothing will ask, or tell us;
She stands on no terms,
  Nor chaffers by way of Indenture;
Nor loves for your Farms,
  But takes the kind man at adventure;
If all prove not right,
  Without act, process, or warning;
From a Wife for a night
  You may be divorc'd in the morning;
Where Parents are slaves,
  Their Brats cannot be any other:
Great Wits, and great Braves
  Have alwaies a Punck for their Mother.

"OUR PARENTS COME TOGETHER FIRST"

[*c.* 1674]

[From *Bristol Drollery*, p. 95].

Our Parents come together first,
To satisfie each others Lust;
Pleasure is the main procurer,
And Matrmony's best insurer:
Other ends they scarce have any,
Though they do pretend to many.
Thus we're got, and as they before,
We soon are ripe for getting more.
Come, *Phillis*, then let's try our skill,
And Dame Nature's Laws fulfill.
The world will quickly desart lye,
If we each other should deny.
Come, what afraid art to surrender,
Because thou art yet young and tender.
    I'le gently handle thee, my Joy,
    With ease we'l try to get a boy,
    And pleasures that shall never cloy.

"WHEN FLORA HAD ON HER NEW GOWN"

[*c.* 1674]

[From *Bristol Drollery*, p. 86].

When Flora had on her new Gown a,
And each pretty flower was blown a,
    E're the Scyth cut the grass,
    I met a pretty Lass,
And I gave her a dainty green Gown a.

She got up again, and did frown a,
And call'd me both Coxcomb and Clown a,
    'Cause I kiss'd lip and cheek,
    T'other thing did not seek,
When I had her so featly there down a.

'Twixt anger and shame then a blush a,
Came over my face with a flush a;
    But what I lost on the grass
    Like a good natur'd Lass,
She afforded me under a Bush a.

"COME PHILLIS, LET'S PLAY"

[*c.* 1674]

[From *Bristol Drollery*, p. 89].

Come *Phillis*, let's play,
  What though it be day,
There's something we have yet to do,
  Shall make thee confess
  There's no end to our bliss,
But ever our pleasures renew.

Thou hast so much treasure
  Exceeding all measure,
And here I've been so long a stranger,
  On this Snowy white hill
  I shall ne'r have my fill,
But o're it cou'd still be a ranger.

Oh here's such a Waste
  A Smock that is lac'd.
And a Bosome much whiter is seen;
  Below which there lies
  Such delicate Thighs,
And that shall be nameless between.

But above all a Face,
And a Head in a Lace
O'er which such a glory do's shine;
That in pleasure I swim
On a bright Cherubim,
For my *Phillis* is sure as divine.

E're all thy sweets be enjoy'd,
Or I shall be cloy'd,
An age will be past, and time shall away;
Whil'st our Play do's go on
With the rise of each Sun,
And night shall begin but the sports of the Day.

"THE SPORTS ON THE GREEN ETC."

[*c.* 1674]

[From *Bristol Drollery*, p. 52].

The Sports on the green we'l leave to the Swains,
The rise of their loves, and reward of their pains;
At the Tavern we'l dine, then close up the day,
At night, at a Mask, a Ball, or a Play.
  And when this is done we laugh and lie down,
  And our Evening delights sweet slumbers shall
    crown.

At the Pell we will play, or a race we will run,
We'l sport with the racket, and when that is done,
At Cribbidge, at In, or at Hazard amain,
From Tick or Baggamon we will not refrain:
  And when we have done, we'l laugh and lie
    down,
  And our passed delights sweet slumber shall
    crown.

Then we'l away to the Gardens or Park,
With Lures for the Ladies, instead of the Lark,
With graces attractive, are fetch'd from Love's Mine

And his darts shall secure us the prey we design.
  And when we have done, we'l laugh and lie down,
  And dream of our Loves, enjoyment shall crown.

With the delicate Nymphs we'l toy and we'l kiss,
So long till we find they will yield to'ther bliss;
We'l tempt pretty *Susan,* and *Marg'ret,* and *Jenny,*
For midnight access, with the bribe of a *Guiney;*
  And when we have done, we'l strip and lie down,
  And then with enjoyment our Loves we will
    crown.

"AMYNTAS HAD PHILIS FAST LOCK'D IN HIS ARMS"

[*c.* 1674]

[From *Bristol Drollery*, p. 8].

Amyntas had Philis fast lock'd in his arms,
But night from *Amyntas* hid *Phillis's* charms.
He clipt, and he kist, and he kist her again,
While she lay twinkling 'twixt pleasure and pain:
But still between kissing *Amyntas* did say,
Fair *Philis*, look up, and you'l turn Night to Day.

But *Philis* cry'd, oh! no, I cannot look on thee,
Day will too soon appear, now fie upon thee;
For *Philis* her blushes was loth to discover,
But for each kiss he gave her, she gave him another:
Yet still between kissing *Amyntas* did say, &c.

"ONE EVENING TO KISS"

[*c.* 1674]

[From *Bristol Drollery*, p. 57].

One Evening to kiss
I walk'd with my Miss,
And strait to a Grove we came;
Where in the cool shade
We sported and plai'd
And eased us of our flame,
But oh, then how her eyes did discover,
The delight she receiv'd from her Lover.

The Dew 'gan to fall
And the night birds to call,
So homewards went *Chloris* and I,
To speak of our Joyes,
And such other toyes,
Would make your Love Passions run high:
But oh, how her eyes her delight did discover,
While I plaid the part of a hot-metled Lover.

THE HASTY BRIDEGROOM:

OR

THE RAREST SPORT THAT HATH BEEN TRY'D, BETWEEN A LUSTY BRIDEGROOM AND HIS BRIDE

[1674-81]

[From *Roxburgh Ballads*, ii. 208; tune, *Bass his carrier;* or, *Bow Bells;* see *Pills to Purge Melancholy* (1720), vi. 198].

Come from the Temple, away to the Bed,
As the Merchant transports home his Treasure;
Be not so coy Lady, since we are wed,
'Tis no Sin to taste of the Pleasure:
Then come let us be
blith, merry and free,
Upon my life all the waiters are gone;
And 'tis so,
that they know
where you go
say not so,
For I mean to make bold with my own.

What is it to me, though our Hands joyned be,
If our Bodies are still kept asunder:
It shall not be said, there goes a marry'd Maid,
Indeed we will have no such wonder:

Therefore let's imbrace,
there's none sees thy Face,
The Bride-Maids that waited are gone;
None can spy
how you lye,
ne'er deny
but say I,
For I mean to make bold with my own.

Then come let us Kiss, and taste of that bliss,
Which brave Lords and Ladies injoy'd;
If Maidens should be of the humour of thee,
Generations would soon be destroy'd:
Then where were those Joys,
the Girls and the Boys,
Would'st live in the World all alone;
Don't destroy,
but enjoy
seem not Coy
for a Toy,
For indeed I'll make bold with my own.

Sweet Love do not frown, but put off thy gown,
'Tis a Garment unfit for the Night;
Some say that Black, hath a relishing smack,
I had rather be dealing in White:
Then be not afraid,
for you are not betray'd,
Since we two are together alone;

I invite
you this Night,
to do right,
my delight
Is forthwith to make use of my own.

Prithee begin, don't delay but unpin,
For my Humour I cannot prevent it;
You are strait lac'd, and your Gorget's so fast,
Undo it, or I straight will rend it:
Or to end all the strife,
I'll cut it a Knife,
'Tis too long to stay 'till it's undone;
Let thy Waste
be unlac'd,
and in hast
be embrac'd,
For I do long to make bold with my own.

Feel with your hand how you make me to stand,
Even ready to starve in the cold,
Oh why shouldst thou be, so hard-hearted to me,
That loves thee more dear than gold
And as thou hast been,
like fair *Venus* the Queen,
Most pleasant in thy parts every one,
let me find,
that thy mind
is inclin'd

to be kind,
So that I may make bold with my own.

As thou art fair, and more sweet than the air,
That dallies on *July's* brave Roses;
Now let me be to that Garden a Key,
That the Flowers of Virgins incloses:
And I will not be
too rough unto thee,
For my Nature unto boldness is prone;
Do no less
than undress,
and unlace
all apace,
For this Night I'll make use with my own.

When I have found thee temperate and sound,
Thy sweet breast I will make for my pillow
'Tis pity that we which newly married be,
Should be forced to wear the green willow;
We shall be blest
and live sweetly at rest,
Now we are united in one:
With content
and consent
I am bent,
my intent
Is this Night to make use of my own.

THE LADIES LOVING REPLY

Welcome dear love, all the powers above,
Are well pleased of our happy meeting
The Heavens have decreed, & the Earth is agreed
That I should imbrace my own sweeting,
At bed and at board
both in deed and in word
My affection to thee shall be shown:
Thou art mine,
I am thine,
Let us joyn,
and combine,
I'll not bar thee from what is thy own.

Our Bride-beds made, thou shalt be my comrade
For to lodge in my arms all the night,
Where thou shalt enjoy, being free from annoy
All the sports wherein love takes delight.
Our mirth shall be crown'd,
and our triumph renown'd,
Then sweetheart let thy valour be shown,
Take thy fill,
do thy will,
use thy skill,
Welcome still,
Why should'st thou not make bold with thy own.

The Bridegroom and Bride, with much joy on
each side
Then together to bed they did go,
But what they did there, I did neither see not hear,
Nor do I desire not to know,
But by Cupids aid,
they being well laid,
They made sport by themselves all alone,
Being plac'd,
and unlac'd,
He uncas'd,
She imbrac'd,
Then he stoutly made use of his own.

YOUNG PHAON

[*c.* 1679]

[From *Choice Ayres & Songs* (JOHN PLAYFORD), ii. (1679); set by JOHN BANNISTER].

Young Phaon strove the Bliss to taste;
  But Sappho still deny'd;
She struggled long, the youth at last,
  Lay panting by her side.
Useless he lay, Love would not wait,
  'Till they could both agree;
They idely languish'd in debate,
  When they should active be.

At last, come ruin me, she cry'd,
  And then there fell a Tear:
I'le in thy Breast my Blushes hide,
  Do all that Virgins fear.
O, that age could loves Rites perform,
  We make Old Men obey;
They court us long, Youth does but storm,
  And plunder and away.

"AT NOON IN A SULTRY SUMMER'S DAY"

[*c.* 1682]

[By the EARL OF DORSET; music in *Pills to Purge Melancholy* (1709), iv. 63; set by J. WELDON].

At Noon in a sultry Summer's Day,
The brightest Lady of the May,
Young Chloris Innocent and Gay,
Sat Knotting in a shade:
Each slender Finger play'd its part,
With such activity and Art;
As wou'd inflame a Youthful Heart,
And warm the most decay'd.

Her Fav'rite Swain by chance came by;
She had him quickly in her Eye,
Yet when the bashful Boy drew nigh,
She wou'd have seem'd afraid,
She let her Iv'ry Needle fall,
And hurl'd away the twisted Ball;
Then gave her Strephon such a call,
As wou'd have wak'd the Dead.

Dear gentle Youth is't none but thee?
With Innocence I dare be free;

By so much Trust and Modesty,
No Nymph was e'er betray'd,
Come lean thy Head upon my Lap,
While thy soft Cheeks I stroak and clap;
Thou may'st securely take a Nap,
Which he poor Fool, obey'd.

She saw him Yawn, and heard him Snore,
And found him fast a sleep all o're;
She Sigh'd——and cou'd no more,
But starting up she said,
Such Vertue shou'd rewarded be,
For this thy dull Fidelity;
I'll trust thee with my Flocks, not me,
Pursue thy Grazing Trade.

Go milk thy Goats, and Sheer thy Sheep,
And watch all Night thy Flocks, to keep;
Thou shalt no more be lull'd asleep,
By me mistaken Maid.

"THE NIGHT HER BLACKEST SABLE WORE"

[*c.* 1682]

[Attributed to T. DURFEY; *Pills to Purge Melancholy* (1707), i. 202; and also to SEMPLE OF BELTREES; see *Roxburgh Ballads* (Ballad Soc. Rept.), i. 197].

The Night her blackest Sable wore,
  And gloomy were the Skies;
And glitt'ring Stars there were no more,
  Than those in *Stella's* Eyes:
When at her Father's Gate I knock'd,
  Where I had often been,
And Shrowded only with her Smock,
  The Fair one let me in.

Fast lock'd within her close Embrace,
  She trembling lay asham'd;
Her swelling Breast, and glowing Face,
  And every touch inflam'd:
My eager Passion I obey'd,
  Resolv'd the Fort to win;
And her fond Heart was soon betray'd,
  To yield and let me in.

Then! then! beyond expressing,
  Immortal was the Joy;
I knew no greater blessing,
  So great a God was I:
And she transported with delight,
  Oft pray'd me come again;
And kindly vow'd that every Night,
  She'd rise and let me in.

But, oh! at last she prov'd with Bern,
  And sighing sat and dull;
And I that was as much concern'd,
  Look'd then just like a Fool:
Her lovely Eyes with tears run o'er,
  Repenting her rash Sin;
She sigh'd and curs'd the fatal hour,
  That e'er she let me in.

But who could cruelly deceive,
  Or from such Beauty part;
I lov'd her so, I could not leave
  The Charmer of my Heart:
But Wedded and conceal'd the Crime,
  Thus all was well again;
And now she thanks the Blessed Hour,
  That e'er she let me in.

THE GELDING THE DEVIL

[*c.* 1682]

[From *Pills to Purge Melancholy* (1709), iv. 115; set by THOMAS WROTH].

I met with the Devil in the shape of a Ram,
Then over and over the Sow-gelder came;
I rose and halter'd him fast by the Horns,
And pick'd out his Stones, as you would pick out Corns;
Maa, quoth the Devil, with that out he slunk,
And left us a Carkass of Mutton that stunk.

I chanc'd to ride forth a Mile and a half,
Where I heard he did live in disguise of a Calf;
I bound him and gelt him e'er he did any evil,
For he was at the best but a young sucking Devil:
Maa, yet he cries, and forth he did steal,
And this was sold after for excellent Veal.

Some half a Year after in the Form of a Pig,
I met with the Rogue, and he look'd very big;
I caught at his Leg, laid him down on a Log,

E'er a Man could Fart twice, I made him a Hog:
Huh, huh, quoth the Devil, and gave such a Jerk,
That a Jew was Converted and eat of that Pork.

In Woman's attire I met him most fine,
At first sight I thought him some Angel divine;
But viewing his crab Face I fell to my Trade,
I made him forswear ever acting a Maid:
Meaw, quoth the Devil, and so ran away,
Hid himself in a Fryer's old Weeds as they say.

I walked along and it was my good chance,
To meet with a Black-coat that was in a Trance:
I speedily grip'd him and whip'd off his Cods,
'Twixt his Head and his Breech, I left little odds;
O, quoth the Devil, and so away ran,
Thou oft will be curst by many a Woman.

THE OLD MAN AND YOUNG WIFE

[*c.* 1682]

[From *Wit and Mirth* (1682), p. 17].

There was an Old-man and a Jolly Old-man
  Come love me whereas I lay,
And he would marry a fair young Wife
  The clean contrary way.

He Woo'd her to wed, to wed,
  Come love me whereas I lay,
And after she kick't him out of the bed
  The clean contrary way.

Then for her dinner she looked due,
  Come love me whereas I lay,
Or she would make her Husband rue
  The clean contrary way.

She proved a gallant Houswife soon,
  Come love me whereas I lay,
She was every morning up by noon
  The clean contrary way.

She made him go wash and wring,
  Come love me whereas I lay,
And every day to Dance and Sing
  The clean contrary way.

She made him do a worse thing than this,
  Come love me whereas I lay,
To Father a Child was none of his
  The clean contrary way.

THE BULL'S FEATHER

[*c.* 1682]

[From *Wit and Mirth* (1682), p. 34].

It chanc'd not long ago, as I was walking,
  An Eecho did bring me where two were a talking,
'Twas a man said to his wife, Dye I had rather,
  Then to be cornuted and wear the *Bulls Feather.*

Then presently she reply'd, Sweet art thou jealous?
  Thou canst not play *Vulcan* before I play *Venus;*
Thy fancies are Foolish, such follies to gather:
  There's many an honest man has worn the
    Bulls Feather.

Though it be invisible let no man it scorn,
  Though it be a new Feather made of all old
    horn;
He that disdains it in heart or mind either,
  May be the more subject to wear the *Bulls*
    Feather.

He that lives in discontent or dispair,
  And feareth false measure because his wife's fair,

His thoughts are Inconstant, much like to Winter weather
  Though one or two want it, he shall have a Feather.

Bulls Feathers are common, as *Ergo* in Schools,
  And only contemned by these that are Fools;
Why should a *Bulls Feather* cause any unrest,
  Since Neighbours Fare always is counted the best?

Those Women wh'are Fairest, are likely to give it,
  And Husbands that have them, are apt to believe it;
Some men though their Wives should seem for to Tedder,
  They would play the Kind Neighbour and give the *Bulls Feather.*

Why should we repine, that our Wives are so Kind,
  Since we that are Husbands are of the same mind;
Shall we give them *Feathers* and think to go free,
  Believe it, Believe it, that hardly will be.

For he that disdains my *Bulls Feather* to day,
  May light of a Lass that will play him foul play;
There's never a Gallant that treads on Cows Leather,

But he may be cornuted and wear the *Bulls Feather.*

Though Beer of that Brewing I never did drink
Yet be not displeas'd if I speak what I think,
Scarce ten in a Hundred, believe it, believe it,
But either they'l have it, or else they will give it.

Then let me advise all those that do pine,
For fear that false Jealousie shorten their time,
This disease will Torment them worse than a Feaver,
Then let all be contented to wear the *Bulls Feather.*

NEWS AND NO NEWS

[*c.* 1682]

[From *Wit and Mirth* (1682), p. 39].

White Bears are lately come to Town,
That's no News,
And Cuckolds Dogs shall pull them down,
That's no News,
Ten Dozen of Capons sold for a Crown,
Hey ho, that's News indeed.

A Jackanapes at a Merchants dore,
That's no News,
An *Irishman* in an Alehouse score,
That's no News,
A *Gravesend* Barge without a Whore,
Hey ho, that's News indeed.

A Fizling Cur in a Ladies lap,
That's no News,
And Feathers wagging in a Fools Cap,
That's no News,
A Lyon caught in a Mouse-trap
Hey ho, that's News indeed.

A Roring Gallant not to thrive,
That's no News,
A Drone to rob the poor Bees Hive,
That's no News,
A parsons Wife not apt to S——
Hey ho, that's News indeed.

A Taylor brisk in gaudy Clothes,
That's no News,
A *Frenchman* stradling as he goes,
That's no News,
A Drunkard without a Copper-Nose,
Hey ho, that's News indeed.

A Sattin Suite without a Page,
That's no News;
A Rayling Poet or'e the stage,
That's no News;
A Rich man honest in this Age,
Hey ho, that's News indeed.

A Petty-fogger brib'd with fees,
That's no News,
A Welshman cram'd with toasted Cheese,
That's no News,
A Lad and a Lass in Bed to Freeze,
Hey ho, that's News indeed.

A Lawyer to turn Hypocrite,
That's no News;

A Bailiff to Arrest a Knight,
That's no News;
A Court without a Parasite:
Hey ho, that's News indeed.

Before my News be over slipt,
That's no News,
I wish all Knaves from London shipt,
That's no News;
And all the Whores in Bridewell whipt:
Hey ho, 'Twere News indeed.

THE HEALTHS

[*c.* 1682]

[From *Wit and Mirth* (1682), p. 45].

Here's a Health to a merry old Sinner
  A Glass of strong *Aquavitae*,
That for a Crown and a Dinner
  Will get you a Wench will delight you.

Because that you are not for Ale
  Here's a Health to a Wench in strong Beer.
Although she (like it) be stale
  She may happen to cost you dear.

Here's a Health in Ale to your Dear
  That lately serv'd in the Kitchin,
A Bouncing wastcoteer
  A remedy for your itching.

Here's a Health to the Vintners Daughter
  In Rhenish with Lemon and Sugar,
Who (with this well Ballanc'd) will after
  Give you libertie to hug her.

To the green-sickness Maid
  Here's a Health in Sparkling white,

Though she be never so stayd
  She may alter her mind ere night.

To the new married wife
  Here's a Health in neat Clarret,
Though her spouse lead a jealous life
  Her tongue out pratles a Parret.

To the jovial Widow at last
  A Health wee'l drink in Sack,
Her constitution's in hast
  You may quickly guess what she does lack.

Now you have so freely drunk
  These Healths so merrily round,
Each of you may go to his punk
  They're your own a penny to a pound.

But now I've thought better on't
  'Tis best leave Drinking and Whoring,
For virtue hereafter will vant
  When vice shall receive a scowring.

CONSTANT, FAIRE, AND FINE BETTY

BEING THE YOUNG-MAN'S PRAISE OF A CURIOUS CREATURE

Faire shee was, and faire indeed
And constant always did proceed.

[*b.* 1683]

[From *Roxburgh Ballads*, i. 65, 67; by RICHARD CRIMSAL; tune, *Peggy went over Lea with a Souldier*].

Now of my sweet Bettie
  I must speake in praise,
I never did see
  such a lasse in my days:
She is kind and loving,
  and constant to me:
Wherefore I will speake
  of my pretty Betty.

Betty is comely,
  and Betty is kind;
Besides, shee is pretty,
  and pleaseth my mind:

She is a brave bonny Lasse,
lovely and free;
The best that ere was
is my pretty Betty.

Her haire it doth glister
like to threeds of gold;
All those that doe meet her
admire to behold:
Her they take for Juno,
so glorious seemes shee,
More brighter than Lun[a]
is pretty Betty.

Her eyes they do twinkle
like starres in the skie;
She is without wrinkle;
her fore-head is high:
Faire Venus for beauty
the like cannot be;
Thus I show my duty
to pretty Betty.

She hath fine cherry cheekes
and sweet corrall lips:
There is many one seekes
love with kisses and clips
But she, like Diana,
flies their company;

She is my Tytana,
  my pretty Bettie.

Her chinne it is dimpled,
  her visage is faire;
She is finely templed;
  she is neat and rare:
If Hellen were living
  she could not please me;
I ioy in praise giving
  my pretty Betty.

Her skinne white as snow,
  her brest soft as doune,
All her parts below
  they are all firme and sound:
Shee's chaste in affection
  as Penelope.
Thus ends the complexion
  of pretty Bettie.

THE SECOND PART, TO THE SAME TUNE

Now of her conditions
  something Ile declare,
For some have suspitions
  she's false being faire:
But shee's not false hearted
  in any degree;

I'm glad I consorted
  with pretty Betty.

Her words and her actions
  they are all as one,
And all her affection
  is on me alone:
She hates such as vary
  from true constancy;
Long I must not tarry
  from pretty Betty.

"Well met my sweet hony,
  my ioy and delight.
O how hath my cony
  done ere since last night?
O what saies my dearest,
  what saist thou to me?"
Of all maids the rarest
  is pretty Betté.

Wo. Kind love, thou art welcome
  to me day and night:
Why came you not home?
  I did long for your sight:
My ioy and my pleasure
  is onely in thee;
Thou art all the treasure
  of pretty Betté.

Hadst thou not come quickly
  I thinke I should dye;
For I was growne sickly
  and did not know why.
Now thou art my doctor
  and physicke to me
In love thou art proctor
  for pretty Betté.

Sweet when shall we marry,
  and lodge in one bed?
Long I cannot carry
  not my maidenhead:
And there's none shall have the same,
  but onely thee;
'Tis thee that I crave
  to love pretty Betté.

MAN. Besse, be thou contented,
  wee'l quickly be wed;
Our friends are consented
  to all hath bin sed;
Thou shalt be my wife
  ere much older I be,
And Ile lead my life
  with my pretty Betté.

These lovers were married,
  and immediately:

And all was well carried;
  they liv'd lovingly:
Let faire maids prove constant
  like pretty Besse,
Fine Besse hath the praise [o]n't,
  and worthy is shee.

THE OLD WOMAN'S WISH

[*c.* 1684]

[A Broadside Song; music in *Pills to Purge Melancholy* (1707), iii. 101].

As I went by an Hospital,
  I heard an Old Woman cry,
Kind Sir, quoth she, be kind to me,
  once more before I Die,
And grant to me those Joys,
  that belong to Woman-kind,
And the Fates above reward your Love,
  To an old Woman Poor and Blind.

I find an itching in my Blood,
  altho' it be something Cold,
Therefore Good Man do what you can,
  to comfort me now I'm Old.
      And Grant to me those Joys, &c.

Altho' I cannot see the Day,
  nor never a glance of light;
Kind Sir, I swear and do declare,
  I honour the Joys of Night:
      Then grant to me those Joys, &c.

When I was in my Blooming Youth,
  My vigorous Love was Hot;
Now in my Age I dare Engage,
  A fancy I still have got:
    Then give to me those Joys, &c.

You shall miss of a Reward,
  If Readily you comply;
Then do not Blush but touch my flesh,
  This minute before I die:
    O let me tast those Joys, &c.

I Forty Shillings would freely give,
  'Tis all the Mony I have;
Which I full long have begged for,
  To carry me to my Grave:
    This I would give to have the Bliss, &c.

I had a Husband in my Youth,
  As very well 'tis known,
The truth to tell he pleased me well,
  But now I am left alone;
    And long to tast the good Old Game, &c.

If Forty Shillings will not do,
  My Petticoat and my Gown;
Nay Smock also shall freely go,
  To make up the other Crown;
    Then Sir, pray Grant that kind Request, &c.

Tho' I am Fourscore Years of Age,
  I love with a Right good Will;
And what in truth I want in Youth,
  I have it in perfect Skill:
    Then grant to me that Charming Bliss, &c.

Now if you do not pleasure me,
  And give me the thing I crave;
I do protest I shall not rest,
  When I am laid in my Grave:
    Therefore kind Sir, grant me the Joys, &c.

"SOME FOUR YEARS AGO"

[1689]

[By C. COTTON, *Poems on Several Occasions*, p. 165].

Some four years ago I made *Phillis* an offer,
Provided she would be my Wh . . . re,
Of two thousand good Crowns to put in her Coffer,
And I think should have given her more.

About two years after, a Message she sent me,
She was for a thousand my own,
But unless for an hundred she now would content me,
I sent her word I would have none.

She fell to my price six or seven weeks after,
And then for a hundred would doe;
I then told her in vain she talk'd of the matter,
Than twenty no farther I'd goe.

T'other day for six Ducatoons she was willing,
Which I thought a great deal too dear,
And told her unless it would come for two shilling,
She must seek a Chapman elsewhere.

This Morning she's come, and would fain buckle
gratis,
But she's grown so fulsome a Wh . . . re,
That now methinks nothing a far dearer rate is,
Than all that I offer'd before.

A SONG IN THE COMEDY CALL'D THE OLD BATCHELOUR

[1693]

[From *The Old Batchelour*, by WILLIAM CONGREVE; music in *Pills to Purge Melancholy* (1709), iv. 188; set by Mr. HENRY PURCELL].

As Amoret and Thyrsis lay,
As Amoret and Thyrsis lay;
Melting, melting, melting, melting the Hours in
 gentle play,
Joyning, joyning, joyning Faces, mingling Kisses,
Mingling kisses, mingling kisses, and exchanging
 harmless Blisses:
He trembling cry'd with eager, eager hast,
Let me, let me, let me feed, oh! oh! let me,
 let me,
Let me, let me feed, oh! oh! oh! oh! let me,
 let me, let me, let me Feed as well as Tast,
I dye, dye, dye, I dye, dye, I dye,
I dye, if I'm not wholly Blest.

The fearful Nymph reply'd forbear,
I cannot, dare not, must not hear;

Dearest *Thyrsis* do not move me,
Do not, do not, if you Love me;
O let me still, the Shepherd said,
But while she fond resistance made,
The hasty joy in struggling fled.

Vex'd at the Pleasure she had miss'd,
She frown'd and blush'd, and sigh'd and kiss'd,
And seem'd to moan, in sullen Cooing,
The sad miscarriage of their Wooing:
But vain alas! were all her Charms,
For *Thyrsis* deaf to Love's allarms,
Baffled and fenceless, tir'd her Arms.

THE DISAPPOINTMENT

[*c.* 1697]

[By Mrs. BEHN, *Poems*, 2nd ed., p. 70].

One day the Amorous *Lysander*,
By an impatient Passion sway'd,
Surpris'd fair *Cloris*, that lov'd Maid,
Who could defend herself no longer.
All things did with his Love conspire;
The gilded Planet of the Day,
In his gay Chariot drawn by Fire,
Was now descending to the Sea,
And left no Light to guide the World,
But what from *Cloris* Brighter Eyes was hurld.

In a lone Thicket made for Love,
Silent as yielding Maids Consent,
She with a Charming Languishment,
Permits his Force, yet gently strove;
Her Hands his Bosom softly meet,
But not to put him back design'd,
Rather to draw 'em on inclin'd:
Whilst he lay trembling at her Feet,
Resistance 'tis in vain to show;
She wants the pow'r to say—*Ah! what d'ye do?*

Her Bright Eyes sweet, and yet severe,
Where Love and Shame confus'dly strive,
Fresh Vigor to *Lysander* give;
And breathing faintly in his Ear,
She cry'd—*Cease, Cease—your vain Desire,*
Or I'll call out—What would you do?
My Dearer Honour ev'n to You
I cannot, must not give—Retire,
Or take this Life, whose chiefest part
I gave you with the Conquest of my Heart.

But he as much unus'd to Fear,
As he was capable of Love,
The blessed minutes to improve,
Kisses her Mouth, her Neck, her Hair;
Each Touch her new Desire Alarms,
His burning trembling Hand he prest
Upon her swelling Snowy Brest,
While she lay panting in his Arms.
All her unguarded Beauties lie
The Spoils and Trophies of the Enemy.

And now without Respect or Fear,
He seeks the Object of his Vows,
(His Love no Modesty allows)
His swift degrees advancing—where
His daring Hand that Altar seiz'd,
Where Gods of Love do Sacrifice:
That Awful Throne, the Paradice

Where Rage is calm'd, and Anger pleas'd;
That Fountain where Delight still flows,
And gives the Universal World Repose.

Her Balmy Lips incountring his,
Their Bodies, as their Souls, are joyn'd;
Where both in Transports Unconfin'd
Extend themselves upon the Moss.
Cloris half dead and breathless lay;
Her soft Eyes cast a Humid Light,
Such as divides the Day and Night;
Or falling Stars, whose Fires decay:
And now no signs of Life she shows,
But what in short-breath'd Sighs returns & goes.

He saw how at her Length she lay;
He saw her rising Bosom bare;
Her loose thin *Robes*, through which appear
A Shape design'd for Love and Play;
Abandon'd by her Pride and Shame,
She does her softest joys dispence,
Off'ring her Virgin-Innocence
A Victim to Loves Sacred Flame;
While the o'er-Ravish'd Shepherd lies
Unable to perform the Sacrifice.

Ready to taste a thousand Joys,
The too transported hapless Swain

Found the vast Pleasure turn'd to Pain;
Pleasure which too much Love destroys:
The willing Garments by he laid,
And Heaven all open'd to his view,
Mad to possess, himself he threw
On the Defenceless Lovely Maid.
But Oh what envying God conspires
To snatch his Power, yet leaves him the Desire.

Nature's Support, (without whose Aid
She can no Humane Being give)
It self now wants the Art to live;
Faintness its slack'ned Nerves invade:
In vain th'enraged Youth essay'd
To call its fleeting Vigor back,
No motion 'twill from Motion take;
Excess of Love his Love betray'd:
In vain he toils, in vain Commands;
The insensible fell weeping in his Hand.

In this so Amorous Cruel Strife,
Where Love and Fate were too severe,
The poor *Lysander* in dispair
Renounc'd his Reason with his Life:
Now all the brisk and active Fire
That should the Nobler parts inflame,
Serv'd to increase his Rage and Shame,
And left no spark for New Desire:

Not all her Naked Charms cou'd move
Or calm that Rage that had debauch'd his Love.

Cloris returning from the Trance
Which Love and soft Desire had bred,
Her timerous Hand she gently laid
(Or guided by Design or Chance)
Upon that Famous *Priapas*,
That Potent God, as Poets feign;
But never did young *Shepherdess*,
Gath'ring of Fern upon the Plain,
More nimbly draw her Fingers back,
Finding beneath the verdant Leaves a Snake.

Than *Cloris* her fair Hand withdrew,
Finding that God of her Desires
Disarm'd of all his Awful Fires,
And Cold as Flow'rs bath'd in the Morning Dew.
Who can the Nymph's Confusion guess?
The Blood forsook the hinder Place,
And strew'd with Blushes all her Face,
Which both Disdain and Shame exprest:
And from *Lysander's* Arms she fled,
Leaving him fainting on the Gloomy Bed.

Like Lightning through the Grove she hies,
Or *Daphne* from the *Delphick God*,
No Print upon the grassey Road
She leaves, t'instruct Pursuing Eyes.

The Wind that wanton'd in her Hair,
And with her Ruffled Garments plaid,
Discover'd in the Flying Maid
All that the God e'er made, if Fair.
So *Venus*, when her *Love* was slain,
With Fear and Haste flew o'er the Fatal Plain.

The *Nymphs* resentment none but I
Can well Imagine or Condole:
But none can guess *Lysander's* Soul,
But those who sway'd his Destiny.
His silent Griefts swell up to Storms,
And not one God his Fury spares;
He curs'd his Birth, his Fate, his Stars;
But more the *Shepherdess's* Charms,
Whose soft bewitching Influence
Had Damn'd him to the *Hell* of Impotence.

THE WILLING MISTRESS

[*c.* 1697]

[By APHRA BEHN, *Poems* (1697), p. 44].

Amyntas led me to a Grove,
  Where all the Trees did shade us;
The Sun itself, though it had Strove,
  It could not have betray'd us:
The place secur'd from humane Eyes,
  No other fear allows,
But when the Winds that gently rise,
  Doe Kiss the yielding Boughs.

Down there we satt upon the Moss,
  And did begin to play
A Thousand Amorous Tricks, to pass
  The heat of all the day.
A many Kisses he did give:
  And I return'd the same
Which made me willing to receive
  That which I dare not name.

His Charming Eyes no Aid requir'd
  To tell their softning Tale;
On her that was already fir'd,

'Twas Easy to prevaile.
He did but Kiss and Clasp me round,
Whilst those his thoughts Exprest:
And lay'd me gently on the Ground;
Ah who can guess the rest?

"CHLOE FOUND AMYNTAS LYING"

[*b.* 1700]

[By DRYDEN; music in *Pills to Purge Melancholy* (1707), i. 232].

Chloe found *Amyntas* lying,
  All in Tears upon the Plain:
Sighing to himself and crying,
  Wretched I to love in vain!
Kiss me, kiss me, Dear, before my Dying;
  Kiss me once and ease my pain.

Sighing to himself and crying,
  Wretched I to love in vain;
Ever scorning and denying,
  To reward your faithful Swain:
Kiss me, Dear, before my Dying,
  Kiss me once and ease my pain.

Ever scorning and denying,
  To reward your faithful Swain;
Chloe, laughing at his crying,
  Told him that he Lov'd in vain;
Kiss me, Dear, before my Dying,
  Kiss me once and ease my pain.

Chloe, laughing at his crying,
  Told him that he lov'd in vain;
But repenting and Complying,
  When He Kiss'd, She Kiss'd again:
Kiss'd him up before his Dying,
  Kiss'd him up, and eas'd his pain.

"CHLOE BLUSH'D AND FROWN'D AND SWORE"

[1705]

[From *The Biter*, by NICHOLAS ROWE; music in *Pills to Purge Melancholy* (1709), iv. 162; set by JOHN ECCLES].

Chloe blush'd and frown'd and swore,
  And push'd me rudely from her;
I call'd her Faithless, Jilting VVhore,
  To talk to me of Honour:
But when I rose and wou'd be gone,
  She cry'd nay, whither go ye?
Young *Damon* say, now we're alone,
  Do, do, do what you will, do what you will with *Chloe*:
Do what you will, what you will, what you will with *Chloe*,
Do what you will, what you will, what you will with *Chloe*.

"PHILANDER AND SYLVIA, A GENTLE SOFT PAIR"

[*c.* 1707]

[From NAT. LEE; music in *Pills to Purge Melancholy* (1707), iii. 220].

Philander and *Sylvia*, a gentle soft Pair,
Whose business was loving, and kissing their Care;
In a sweet smelling Grove went smiling along,
'Till the Youth gave a vent to his Heart with his Tongue:
Ah *Sylvia!* said he, (and sigh'd when he spoke)
Your cruel resolves will you never revoke?
No never, she said, how never, he cry'd,
'Tis the Damn'd that shall only that Sentence abide.

She turn'd her about to look all around,
Then blush'd, and her pretty Eyes cast on the Ground;
She kiss'd his warm Cheeks, then play'd with his Neck,
And urg'd that his Reason his Passion would check:

Ah *Philander!* she said, 'tis a dangerous Bliss,
Ah! never ask more and I'll give thee a Kiss;
How never? he cry'd, then shiver'd all o'er,
No never, she said, then tripp'd to a Bower.

She stopp'd at the Wicket, he cry'd, let me in,
She answer'd, I wou'd if it were not a sin;
Heav'n sees, and the Gods will chastise the poor
Head
Of *Philander* for this; straight Trembling he said,
Heav'n sees, I confess, but no Tell-tales are there,
She kiss'd him and cry'd, you're an Atheist my
Dear;
And shou'd you prove false I should never en-
dure:
How never? he cry'd, and straight down he
threw her.

Her delicate Body he clasp'd in his Arms,
He kiss'd her, he press'd her, heap'd charms upon
charms;
He cry'd shall I now? no never, she said,
Your Will you shall never enjoy till I'm dead:
Then as if she were dead, she slept and lay still,
Yet even in Death bequeath'd him a smile:
Which embolden'd the Youth his Charms to apply,
Which he bore still about him to cure those
that die.

"UPON A SUNSHINE SUMMERS DAY"

[*c.* 1707]

[From *Pills to Purge Melancholy* (1707), i. 115; music, *ibid.*, p. 113].

Upon a sunshine Summers day,
When every Tree was green and gay;
The Morning blusht with Phœbus ray,
Just then ascending from the Sea:
As *Silvia* did a Hunting ride,
A lovely Cottage he espy'd;
Where lovely *Cloe* Spinning sat,
And still she turn'd her Wheel about.

Her Face a Thousand Graces crown,
Her curling Hair was lovely brown;
Her rowling Eyes all Hearts did win,
And white as Down of Swans her Skin:
So taking her plain Dress appears,
Her Age not passing Sixteen Years;
The Swain lay sighing at her Foot,
Yet still she turn'd her Wheel about.

Thou sweetest of thy tender kind,
Cries he, this ne'er can suit thy Mind;

Such Grace attracting noble Loves,
Was ne'er design'd for Woods and Groves:
Come, come with me, to Court my Dear,
Partake my Love and Honour there;
And leave this Rural sordid rout,
And turn no more thy Wheel about.

At this with some few Modest sighs,
She turns to him her Charming Eyes;
Ah! tempt me Sir, no more she cries,
Nor seek my Weakness to surprise:
I know your Art's to be believ'd,
I know how Virgins are deceiv'd;
Then let me thus my Life wear out,
And turn my harmless Wheel about.

By that dear panting Breast cries he,
And yet unseen divinity;
Nay, by my Soul that rests in thee,
I swear this cannot, must not be:
Ah! cause not my eternal woe,
Nor kill the Man that Loves thee so;
But go with me, and ease my doubt,
And turn no more thy Wheel about.

His cunning Tongue so play'd its part,
He gain'd admission to her Heart;
And now she thinks it is no Sin,
To take Loves fatal poison in:

But ah! too late she found her fault,
For he her Charms had soon forgot;
And left her e'er the Year ran out,
In Tears to turn her Wheel about.

"TELL ME NO MORE . . . I AM DECEIV'D"

[*c.* 1707]

[From *Pills to Purge Melancholy* (1707), i. 285].

Tell me no more, no more, I am deceiv'd
  That *Cloe's* false, that *Cloe's* false and common;
By Heav'n I all along believ'd,
  She was, she was, a very, very Woman.
As such I lik'd, as such carest,
  She still, she still was constant when possest:
She cou'd, she cou'd, she cou'd, she cou'd
  Do more for no Man.

But oh! but oh her Thoughts on others ran,
  And that you think, and that you think a hard
    thing;
Perhaps she fancy'd you the Man,
  Why what care I, what care I one Farthing.
You say she's false, I'm sure she's kind,
  I'll take, I'll take her Body, you her Mind;
Who, who has the better Bargain?

"WHEN FIRST AMYNTAS SU'D FOR A KISS"

[*c.* 1707]

[From *Pills to Purge Melancholy* (1707), i. 274].

When first *Amyntas* su'd for a Kiss,
  My innocent Heart was tender;
That tho' I push'd him away from the bliss,
  My Eyes declar'd my Heart was won;
I fain an artful Coyness wou'd use,
  Before I the Fort did Surrender:
But Love wou'd suffer no more such abuse,
  And soon, alas! my cheat was known:
He'd sit all day, and laugh and play,
  A thousand pretty things would say;
My hand he'd squeez, and press my knees,
  Till farther on he got by degrees.

My Heart, just like a Vessel at Sea,
  Wou'd toss when *Amyntas* was near me;
But ah! so cunning a Pilot was he,
  Thro' Doubts and Fears he'd still sail on:
I thought in him no danger cou'd be,
  Too wisely he knows how to steer me;

And soon, alas! was brought to agree,
To tast of Joys before unknown:
Well might he boast his Pain not lost,
For soon he found the Golden Coast;
Enjoy'd the Oar, and 'tach'd the shore,
Where never Merchant went before.

"I TELL THEE DICK WHERE I HAVE BEEN"

[*c.* 1707]

[From *Pills to Purge Melancholy* (1707), i. 150].

I tell thee *Dick* where I have been,
Where I the rarest things have seen,
O things beyond compare;
Such sights again cannot be found,
In any place on English ground,
Be it at Wake or Fair.

At Charing Cross, hard by the way,
Where we (thou know'st) do sell our Hay,
There is a House with Stairs;
And there did I see coming down,
Such Voulks as are not in our Town,
Vorty at least in pairs.

Amongst the rest one Pestilent fine,
(His Beard no bigger tho' than thine)
Walkt on before the rest;
Our Landlord lookt like nothing to him,

The King (God bless him) 'twould undo him,
Should he go still so drest.

At course-a-Park without all doubt,
He should have first been taken out,
By all the Maids i'th' Town;
Tho' lusty *Roger* there had been,
Or little *George* upon the green,
Or *Vincent* of the Crown.

But wot you what, the Youth was going,
To make an end of his own Wooing,
The Parson for him stay'd;
Yet by his leave (for all his hast)
He did not so much Wish all past,
Perchance as did the Maid.

The Maid (and thereby hangs a Tale)
For such a Maid no Whitson Ale,
Could ever yet produce;
No Grape that's kindly ripe could
So round, so plump, so soft as she,
Nor half so full of Juice.

Her Fingers was so small, the Ring,
Would not stay on, which he did bring,
It was too wide a Peck;
And to say Truth, (for out it must)
It lookt like the great Coller (just)
About our young Colt's Neck.

Her Feet beneath her Petticoat,
Like little Mice stole in and out,
As if they fear'd the Light;
But *Dick*, she Dances such away,
No Sun upon a Easter day,
Is half so fine a sight.

He would have kist her once or twice,
But she would not she was so nice,
She would not do it in Sight;
And then she lookt, as who would say,
I will do what I list to Day,
And you shall do't at Night.

Her Cheeks so rare a white was on,
No Dazy makes Comparison,
(Who sees them is undone,)
For streaks of red were mingled there,
Such as are on a Katherine Pear,
The side that's next the Sun.

Her lips were red, and one was thin,
Compar'd to that was next her Chin;
(Some Bee had stung it newly:)
But (*Dick*) her Eyes so guard her Face,
I durst no more upon them gaze,
Than on the Sun in July.

Her Mouth so small when she does speak,
Thou'dst swear her Teeth her Words did break,

That they might passage get;
But she so handled still the matter,
They came as good as ours, or better,
And are not spent a whit.

If wishing should be any Sin,
The Parson himself had guilty been,
She lookt that Day so purely,
And did the Youth so oft the Feat,
At Night, as some did in Conceit,
It would have spoil'd him surely.

Passion, oh me! how I run on!
There's that that would be thought upon,
(I trow) besides the Bride:
The Business of the Kitchin's great,
For it is fit that Man should eat;
Nor was it there deny'd.

Just in the Nick the Cook knockt thrice,
And all the Waiters in a trice
His Summons did obey,
Each Serving-man with Dish in Hand
March'd boldly up, like our train'd Band,
Presented, and away.

When all the Meat was on the Table,
What Man of Knife, or Teeth was able
To stay to be intreated;

And this very reason was,
Before the Parson could say Grace,
The Company was seated.

Now Hats fly off, and Youths carouse,
Healths first go round, and then the House,
The Brides came thick and thick;
And when 'twas nam'd another's Health,
Perhaps he made it hers by Stealth;
And who could help it *Dick*?

O'th' sudden up they rise and dance,
Then sit again, and sigh and glance;
Then dance again and kiss;
Thus sev'ral ways the Time did pass,
Whilst every Woman wish'd her Place,
And every Man wish'd his.

By this Time all was stol'n aside,
To counsel and undress the Bride
But that he must not know:
But 'twas thought he guest her Mind,
And did not mean to stay behind,
Above an Hour or so.

When in he came (*Dick*) there she lay,
Like new fall'n Snow melting away,
('Twas time I trow to part)
Kisses were now the only stay,

Which soon he gave, as who would say
Good B'w'y! with all my Heart.

But just as Heavens would have to cross it,
In came the Bride-maids with the Posset,
The Bridegroom eat in spight;
For had he left the Women to't,
It would have cost two Hours to do't,
Which were too much that Night.

At length the Candle's out, and now,
All that they had not done they do;
What that is, you can tell;
But I believe it was no more,
Than thou and I have done before,
With *Bridget*, and with *Nell*.

A BALLAD OF OLD PROVERBS

[*c.* 1707]

[From *Pills to Purge Melancholy* (1707), ii. 112].

I prithee Sweet-heart grant me my desire,
  For I am thrown as the old *Proverb* goes,
Out of the Frying-pan, into the Fire,
  And there is none that Pities my Woes.
Then hang or drown thy self, my Muse,
For there is not a T—d to chuse.

Most Maids prove Coy of late, tho' they seem
    Holier,
  Yet I believe they are all of a Mind;
Like unto like, quoth the Devil to the Collier,
  And they'll be true when the Devil is Blind:
Let no one trust to their desire,
For the burnt Child still dreads the Fire.

What tho' my Love as white as a Dove is,
  Yet you would say, if you knew all within;
Shitten come Shite the beginning of Love is,
  And for her Favour I care not a Pin:

No Love of mine she e'er shall be,
Sir-Reverence of her Company.

What tho' her Disdainfulness my Heart hath cloven,
  Yet I am of so stately a Mind;
I'll not creep in her A— to bake in her Oven,
  Tho' 'tis an old Proverb, that Cat will to kind:
But I will say until I die,
Farewell and be hang'd, that's twice Good-bye.

Alas, no Enjoyments, nor Comfort I can take,
  In her that regards not the worth of a Lover;
A T— is as good for a Sow, as a Pancake:
  Swallow that Gudgeon, I'll Fish for another,
She ne'er regards my aking Heart,
Tell a Mare a Tale, she'll let a Fart.

Now I'm sure as my Shoe is made of Leather,
  Without good advisement and fortunate helps;
We two shall ne'er set our Horses together,
  For she's like a Bear being rob'd of her Whelps:
But as for me it shall ne'er be said,
You've brought an old House over your Head.

Lo, this is my Counsel to young Men that Wooe,
  Look well before you leap, handle your Geer;
For if you Wink and Shite, you'll ne'er see what
    you do,
  So you may take a wrong Sow by the Ear

But if she prove her self a Flurt,
Then she may do as does my Shirt.

Fall Back, or fall Edge, I never shall bound be,
  To make a Match with Tag-rag, and Long-tail;
He that's born to hang, never shall drown'd be,
  Best is best cheap, if you hit not the Nail:
Shall I toil Gratis in the Dirt,
First she shall do as does my Shirt.

"BRING OUT YOUR CONEY-SKINS"

[*c.* 1709]

[From *Pills to Purge Melancholy* (1709), iv. 80].

Bring out your Coney-Skins
  Bring out your Coney-Skins Maids to me,
And hold them fair, fair that I may see,
Grey, Black and Blue, for the smaller Skins
I'll give you Bracelets, Laces, Pins,
    And for your whole Coney
    Here's ready Money,
Come gentle *Joan*, do thou begin
With thy black Coney, thy black Coney-Skin,
    And *Mary* and *Joan* will follow,
    With their Silver-hair'd Skins and yellow;
The White Coney-Skin I will not lay by,
For tho' it be faint, it is fair to the Eye:
The Grey it is worn, but yet for my Money,
Give me the bonny, bonny black Coney;
Come away fair Maids, your Skins will decay,
Come and take Money Maids, put your Wares away:
Ha'ye any Coney-Skins, ha'ye any Coney-Skins,
Ha'ye any Coney-Skins here to sell?

"AH! FOOLISH LASS, WHAT MUN I DO?"

[*c.* 1711]

[From *Pills to Purge Melancholy* (1719), iv. 106; set by JOHN BARRETT].

Ah! foolish Lass, what mun I do?
My Modesty I well may rue,
  Which of my Joy bereft me;
For full of Love he came,
But out of silly shame,
With pish and phoo I play'd,
To muckle the coy Maid,
  And the raw young Loon has left me.

Wou'd *Jockey* knew how muckle I lue,
Did I less Art, or did he shew,
  More Nature, how bleast I'd be;
I'd not have reason to complain,
That I lue'd now in vain,
Gen he more a Man was,
I'd be less a coy Lass,
  Had the raw young Loon weel try'd me.

THE MAN OF THE TOWN

[*b.* 1713]

[Attributed to ARCH. PITCAIRN; from *Ane Pleasant Garden* (*c.* 1800); edited by C. KIRKPATRICK SHARPE].

Room, room for a man in the town,
  Who takes delight in roaring,
That daily rumbleth up and down,
  And spends the night in whoring.
Who, for the modish name of spark,
  Doth his companions rally,
Comes marching out, raging (in) the dark,
  And sneaks into some alley.

To every maiden that he meets,
  He swears he bears affection,
Contemns the laws of Chastity,
  And boasts a stiff erection;
And yet resolving furder on,
  By some resenting cully,
Is decently run through the lungs,
  And there's an end of bully.

"WULLY AND GEORGY NOW BEATH ARE GEAN"

[*c.* 1719]

[From *Pills to Purge Melancholy* (1719), iii. 297].

Wully and Georgy now beath are gean,
To see their lovely Flocks a feeding;
Jenny and Moggy too follow'd them,
For fear they should be now a breeding:
Out of London Town they aw did trip it,
Down to play at new bepeep at Tunbridge Well;
But how they play'd, or what they said,
The De'el his sell can only tell.

Moggy had Bearns, Four, Five or Six,
But Jenny was a young beginner;
Sure to her Trading now she will fix,
The Kirk has made her a young Sinner:
To London Town they're gean,
Each with a muckle Weam:
And Georgy now to Scotland he mun run,
Fare him weel, ene take him De'el,
Poor Jenny now is quite undone.

"FARWEEL BONNY WULLY CRAIG"

[*c.* 1719]

[From *Pills to Purge Melancholy* (1719), iv. 230].

Farweel bonny Wully Craig,
  Farweel to au thy broken Vows to me;
Thou wast a lovely Lad,
  When on the Grass thou tempted'st me:
Full oft have I dry'd mine Eyn,
  When by my seln to Milking I have gean
Oft have I gist the Green,
  Where Wully vow'd to be my Swain.

Sea neat was my conny Lad,
  With new Russet Shoon, and Holland Band;
But now he's won his way,
  With Maiden-head, and Leve and au:
His locks were sea finely scam'd
  And shone as bright as any in the Land;
But now he's won his way,
  With Maiden-head, and Leve and au.

Ise ene thraw away my Skeel,
  And gang nea mere to yonder fatal Brow;

Where I was pleas'd sea weel,
  But now I feel meer ner others do:
He took me by the wulling Hand,
  And vow'd to Hea'n how he wad constant be;
When levingly we laid
  Under the shade of the Wullow-tree.

But ah! when the Loon had deun,
  He nothing more of Love cou'd shew;
But now he's won his way,
  VVith Maiden-head, and Leve and au:
My VVeam now begins to fill,
  And seun the bonny Bird will crow:
Tho' he was won his way,
  VVith Maiden-head, and Leve and au.

THE CRAFTY CRACKS OF EAST-SMITHFIELD, WHO PICK'T UP A MASTER COLOUR UPON TOWER-HILL, WHOM THEY PLUNDRED OF A PURSE OF SILVER, WITH ABOVE THREESCORE GUINEAS

[*c.* 1719]

[From *Pills to Purge Melancholy* (1719), v. 22].

You Master Colliers pray draw near,
  And listen to my Report;
My Grief is great, for lo of late,
  Two Ladies I chanc'd to Court:
Who did meet me on Tower-Hill,
  Their Beauties I did behold:
Those Crafty Jades have learnt their Trades,
  And plunder'd me of my Gold.

I'll tell you how it came to pass,
  This sorrowful Story is thus:
Of Guineas bright a glorious Sight,
  I had in a Cat-skin Purse:

The value of near Fourscore Pounds,
  As good as e'er I had told,
Those Crafty Jades have learnt their Trades,
  And plunder'd me of my Gold.

I saw two poor distressed Men,
  VVho lay upon Tower-Hill,
To whom in brief I gave Relief,
  According to my good VVill:
Two wanton Misses drawing near,
  My Guineas they did behold;
They laid a Plot by which they Got,
  My Silver and yellow Gold.

They both address'd themselves to me,
  And thus they was pleas'd to say:
Kind Sir, indeed, we stand in need,
  Altho' we are fine and gay:
Of some Relief which you may give,
  I thought they were something bold;
The Plot was laid, I was betray'd,
  And plunder'd of all my Gold.

Alas 'tis pity, then I cry'd,
  Such Ladies of good Repute,
Should want Relief, therefore in brief,
  I gave 'em a kind Salute;
Thought I of them I'll have my VVill,
  Altho' I am something old;

They were I see too wise for me,
  They plunder'd me of my Gold.

Then to East-Smithfield was I led,
  And there I was entertain'd:
With Kisses fine and Brandy Wine,
  In Merriment we remain'd:
Methought it was the happiest Day,
  That ever I did behold;
Sweet Meat alass! had sower Sauce,
  They plunder'd me of my Gold.

Time after Time to pay their Shot,
  My Guineas I would lug out;
Those Misses they wou'd make me stay,
  And rally the other bout:
I took my Fill of Pleasures then
  Altho' I was something old;
Those Joys are past, they would not last,
  I'm plunder'd of all my Gold.

As I was at the wanton Game,
  My Pocket they fairly pick'd;
And all my Wealth they took by stealth,
  Thus was a poor Colour trick'd:
Let me therefore a Warning be,
  To Merchants both young and old;
For now of late hard was my Fate,
  I'm plunder'd of all my Gold.

They got three Pounds in Silver bright,
  And Guineas above Threescore,
Such sharping Cracks breaks Merchants Backs,
  I'll never come near them more:
Sure now I have enough of them,
  My Sorrow cannot be told;
That crafty Crew makes me look Blew,
  I'm plunder'd of all my Gold.

"O LET NO EYES BE DRY"

[*c.* 1719]

[From *Pills to Purge Melancholy* (1719), v. 130; "a ballad made by a Gentleman in Ireland, who could not have access to a Lady whom he went to visit, because the maid the night before had overlaid her pretty Bitch; tune, *O Hone, O Hone?*"].

Oh! let no Eyes be dry,
 Oh Hone, Oh Hone,
But let's lament and cry,
 Oh Hone, Oh Hone,
We're quite undone almost,
For Daphne on this Coast,
Has yielded up the Ghost,
 Oh Hone, Oh Hone.

Daphne my dearest Bitch,
 Oh Hone, Oh Hone,
Who did all Dogs bewitch,
 Oh Hone, Oh Hone,
Was by a careless Maid,
Pox take her for a Jade,

In the Night over-laid,
  Oh Hone, Oh Hone.

Oh may she never more
  Oh Hone, Oh Hone,
Sleep quietly, but snore,
  Oh Hone, Oh Hone,
May never Irish Lad,
Sue for her Maiden-head,
Until it stinks I Gad,
  Oh Hone, Oh Hone.

Oh may she never keep
  Oh Hone, Oh Hone;
Her Water in her Sleep,
  Oh Hone, Oh Hone:
May never Pence nor Pounds,
Come more within the Bounds,
Of her Pocket Ad-sounds,
  Oh Hone, Oh Hone.

TO CHUSE A FRIEND, BUT NEVER MARRY

[*c.* 1719]

[From *Pills to Purge Melancholy* (1719), iii. 342].

To all young Men that love to Wooe,
To Kiss and Dance, and Tumble too;
Draw near and Counsel take of me,
Your faithful Pilot I will be:
Kiss who you please, Joan, Kate, or Mary,
But still this Counsel with you carry,
Never Marry.

Court not a Country Lady, she
Knows not how to value thee;
She hath no am'rous Passion, but
What Tray, or Quando has for Slut:
To Lick, to Whine, to Frisk, or Cover,
She'll suffer thee, or any other,
Thus to Love her.

Her Daughter she's now come to Town,
In a rich Linsey Woolsey Gown;
About her Neck a valued Prize,
A Necklace made of Whitings Eyes:

With List for Garters 'bove her Knee,
And Breath that smells of Firmity,
's not for thee.

Of Widows Witchcrafts have a care,
For if they catch you in their Snare;
You must as daily Labourers do,
Be still a shoving with your Plow:
If any rest you do require,
They then deceive you of your Hire,
And retire.

The Maiden Ladies of the Town,
Are scarcely worth your throwing down;
For when you have possession got,
Of Venus Mark, or Hony-pot:
There's such a stir with, marry me,
That one would half forswear to see
Any she.

If that thy Fancy do desire,
A glorious out-side, rich Attire;
Come to the Court, and there you'll find,
Enough of such to Please your Mind:
But if you get too near their Lap,
You're sure to meet with the Mishap,
Call'd a Clap.

With greasy painted Faces drest,
With butter'd Hair, and fucus'd Breast;

Tongues with Dissimulation tipt,
Lips which a Million have them sipp'd:
There's nothing got by such as these,
But Achs in Shoulders, Pains in Knees
For your Fees.

In fine, if thou delight'st to be,
Concern'd in VVomans Company:
Make it the Studies of thy Life,
To find a Rich, young, handsome VVife:
That can with much discretion be
Dear to her Husband, kind to thee,
Secretly.

In such a Mistress, there's the Bliss,
Ten Thousand Joys wrapt in a Kiss;
And in th' Embraces of her VVast,
A Million more of Pleasures taste:
VVho e'er would Marry that could be
Blest with such Opportunity,
Never me.

THE QUEEN OF MAY

[*c.* 1719]

[From *Pills to Purge Melancholy* (1719), iv. 67; tune, *Dancing Master*].

Upon a time I chanced to walk along a Green,
Where pretty Lasses danced in strife to chuse a Queen;
Some homely drest, some handsom, some pretty, and some gay,
But who excell'd in Dancing, must be the Queen of May.

From Morning till the Evening, their Controversy held,
And I, as Judge, stood gazing on, to Crown her that excell'd;
At last when Phœbus Steeds had drawn their Wayn away,
We found and crown'd a Damsel to be the Queen of May.

Full well her Nature from her Face I did admire,
Her Habit well become her, altho' in poor Attire;

Her Carriage was so good, as did appear that Day,
That she was justly chosen to be the Queen of May.

Then all the rest in Sorrow, and she in sweet Content,
Gave over till the Morrow, and homewards strait they went;
But she of all the rest, was hindred by the way,
For ev'ry Youth that met her, must Kiss the Queen of May.

At last I caught and stay'd her a while with me alone,
And on a Bank I laid her, when all the rest were gone;
She fearing some Mischance, cry'd out, forbear I pray,
Yet I could still do nothing but Kiss the Queen of May.

Thus we together tumbled at least an hour or more,
And like a Fool, I Fumbled, as I had done before:
But when that Night was come, by chance I got the day,
And yet alass, did nothing else but Kiss the Queen of May.

Her thoughts of coming thither, both Grief and Joy begot,

She smil'd and wept together, yet knew not well for what,
And still desir'd to go, but yet she seem'd to stay,
  Yet I alas did nothing else but Kiss the Queen of May.

She sigh'd and pray'd for pity that I would once give o'er,
Yet were her Words so Wity, they shew'd she wish'd for more:
Then seeming to defend it, her Fort she did betray;
  Yet I alas did nothing else but Kiss the Queen of May.

Thus shaking Hands at last we part, but she appear'd
Both heavy Ey'd and Hearted, with that she felt and fear'd;
Then turning round we parted, she speechless went her way,
Because I could do nothing but Kiss the Queen of May.

"TO CHARMING CÆLIA'S ARMS I FLEW"

[*c.* 1719]

[From *Pills to Purge Melancholy* (1719), iv. 185].

To Charming Cælia's Arms I flew,
  And there all Night I feasted,
No God such Transport ever knew,
  Or Mortal ever tasted.

Lost in the sweet tumultuous Joy,
  And bless'd beyond Expressing,
How can your Slave, my Fair, said I,
  Reward so great a Blessing?

The whole Creation's Wealth survey,
  O'er both the Indies wander,
Ask what brib'd Senates give away,
  And Fighting Monarchs squander.

The richest Spoils of Earth and Air,
  The rifled Ocean's Treasure,
'Tis all too poor a Bribe by far,
  To purchase so much Pleasure.

She blushing cry'd, my Life, my Dear,
  Since Cælia thus you Fancy,
Give her, but 'tis too much, I fear,
  A Rundlet of right Nantzy.

A CURE FOR MELANCHOLY

[*c.* 1719]

[From *Pills to Purge Melancholy* (1719), v. 118].

Are you grown so Melancholy,
That you think on nought but Folly;
Are you sad,
Are you Mad,
Are you worse;
Do you think,
Want of Chink
Is a Curse:
Do you wish for to have,
Longer Life, or a Grave,
Thus would I Cure ye.

First I would have a Bag of Gold,
That should ten Thousand Pieces hold,
And all that,
In thy Hat,
Would I pour;
For to spend,
On thy Friend,
Or thy Whore:

For to cast away at Dice,
Or to shift you of your Lice,
Thus would I Cure ye.

Next I would have a soft Bed made,
Wherein a Virgin should be laid;
That would Play,
Any way
You'll devise;
That would stick
Like a Tick,
To your Thighs,
That would bill like a Dove,
Lye beneath or above,
Thus would I Cure ye.

Next that same Bowl, where Jove Divine,
Drank Nectar in, I'd fill with Wine;
That whereas,
You should pause,
You should quaff;
Like a Greek,
Till your Cheek,
To Ceres and to Venus,
To Bacchus and Silenus,
Thus would I Cure ye.

Last of all there should appear,
Seven Eunuchs sphere-like Singing here,

In the Praise,
Of those Ways,
Of delights;
Venus can,
Use with Man,
In the Night;
When he strives to adorn,
Vulcan's Head with a Horn,
Thus would I Cure ye.

But if not Gold, nor Woman can,
Nor Wine, nor Songs, make merry then;
Let the Batt,
Be thy Mate,
And the Owl;
Let a Pain,
In thy Brain,
Make thee Howl;
Let the Pox be thy Friend,
And the Plague work thy end,
Thus I would Cure you.

"LUCINDA HAS THE DEVIL AND ALL"

[*c.* 1720]

[From *Pills to Purge Melancholy* (1720), vi. 232].

Lucinda has the de'el and all, the de'el and all, the de'el and all,
Of that bright Thing we Beauty call;
But if she won't come to my Arms,
What care I, why, what care I, what, what care I for all her Charms?
Beauty's the Sauce to Love's high Meat,
But who minds Sauce that must not Eat:
It is indeed a mighty Treasure,
But in using lies the Pleasure;
Bullies thus, that only see't,
Damn all the Gold, damn all the Gold, all, all the Gold in Lombard-street.

"A YOUNG MAN AND A MAID"

[*c.* 1720]

[From *Pills to Purge Melancholy* (1720), vi. 251].

A Young Man and a Maid, put in all, put in all,
Together lately play'd, put in all;
The Young Man was in Jest,
O the Maid she did protest:
She bid him do his best, put in all, put in all.

With that her rowling Eyes, put in all, put in all,
Turn'd upward to the Skies, put in all;
My Skin is White you see,
My Smock above my Knee,
What wou'd you more of me, put in all, put in all.

I hope my Neck and Breast, put in all, put in all,
Lie open to your chest, put in all,
The Young Man was in heat,
The Maid did soundly Sweat,
A little father get, put in all, put in all.

According to her Will, put in all, put in all,
This Young Man try'd his Skill, put in all;

But the Proverb plain does tell,
That use them ne'er so well,
For an Inch they'd take an Ell, put in all, put in all.

When they had ended sport, put in all, put in all,
She found him all too short, put in all;
For when he'd done his best,
The Maid she did protest,
'Twas nothing but a Jest, put in all, put in all.

THE BRITISH ACCOUNTANT

[*c.* 1720]

[From *Pills to Purge Melancholy* (1720), vi. 329].

You Ladies draw near, I can tell you good News,
If you please to give Ear, or else you may
Choose;
Of a British Accountant that's Frolick and free,
Who does wondrous Feats by the Rule of Three.

Addition, Division, and other such Rules,
I'll leave to be us'd by your Scribling Fools;
This Art is Improv'd unto such a Degree,
That he manages all by the Rule of Three.

You Dames that are Wed who can make it
appear,
That you lose an Estate for want of an Heir:
This Accountant will come without e'er a Fee,
And warrants a Boy by his Rule of Three.

Is the Widdow distress'd for the loss of her
Spouse,
Tho' to have him again she cares not a Louse;

Her Wants he supplys whatsoever they be,
And all by his Art in the Rule of Three.

Do you Dream in the Night and fret at your Fate,
For want of the Man when you happen to wake;
You may presently send and satisfy'd be,
That he Pacifies all by the Rule of Three.

You Ladies who are with a Husband unblest,
And are minded to make him a delicate Beast;
He'll fix the Brow-antlers just where they should be,
And all by his Art in the Rule of Three.

You Lasses at large of the true Female Race,
Who are glad of the Men who will lye on their Face;
Do but try the bold Britton, you all will agree,
That you never did know such a Rule of Three.

"ABROAD AS I WAS WALKING"

[*c.* 1720]

[From *Pills to Purge Melancholy* (1720), vi. 247].

Abroad as I was walking, I spy'd two Maids a
wrestling,
The one threw the other unto the Ground;
One Maid she let a Fart, struck the other to
the Heart,
Was not this a grievous Wound?

This Fart it was heard into Mr. Bowman's Yard,
With a great and a mighty Power;
For ought that I can tell, it blew down Bridwell,
And so overcame the Tower.

It blew down Paul's Steeple, and knock'd down
many People,
Alack was the more the pity;
It blew down Leaden-hall, and the Meal-sacks
and all,
And the Meal flew about the City.

It blew down the Exchange, was not this very
strange,
And the Merchants of the City did wound;
This Maid she like a Beast, turn'd her fugo to
the East,
And it roar'd in the Air like Thunder.

THE JOLLY PEDLAR'S PRETTY THING

[*c.* 1720]

[From *Pills to Purge Melancholy* (1720), vi. 248].

A Pedlar proud as I heard tell,
He came into a Town:
With certain Wares he had to sell,
Which he cry'd up and down:
At first of all he did begin,
With Ribbonds, or Laces, Points, or Pins,
Gartering, Girdling, Tape, or Filetting,
Maids any Cunny-skins.

I have of your fine perfumed Gloves,
And made of the best Doe-skin;
Such as young Men do give their Loves,
When they their Favour Win:
Besides he had many a prettier Thing
Than Ribbonds, &c.

I have of your fine Necklaces,
As ever you did behold;
And of your Silk Handkerchiefs,
That are lac'd round with Gold:

Besides he had many a prettier Thing
Than Ribbonds, &c.

Good fellow, says one, and smiling sat,
Your Measure does somewhat Pinch;
Beside you Measure at that rate,
It wants above an Inch:
And then he shew'd her a prettier Thing,
Than Ribbonds, &c.

The Lady was pleas'd with what she had seen,
And vow'd and did protest;
Unless he'd shew it her once again,
She never shou'd be at rest:
With that he shew'd her his prettier Thing
Than Ribbonds, &c.

With that the Pedlar began to huff,
And said his Measure was good,
If that she pleased to try his stuff,
And take it whilst it stood:
And then he gave her a prettier Thing,
Than Ribbonds, &c.

Good fellow said she, when you come again,
Pray bring good store of your Ware;
And for new Customers do not sing,
For I'll take all and to spare:
With that she hugg'd his prettier Thing
Than Ribbonds, &c.

YOUNG STREPHON AND PHILLIS

[*c.* 1720]

[From *Pills to Purge Melancholy* (1720), vi. 220].

Young Strephon and Phillis,
  They sat on a Hill;
But the Shepherd was wanton,
  And wou'd not sit still:
His Head on her Bosom,
  And Arms round her Wast;
He hugg'd her, and kiss'd her,
  And clasp'd her so fast:
'Till playing and jumbling,
  At last they fell tumbling;
And down they got 'em,
But oh! they fell soft on the Grass at the Bottom.

As the Shepherdess tumbled,
  The rude Wind got in,
And blew up her Cloaths,
  And her Smock to her Chin:
The Shepherd he saw
  The bright Venus, he swore,
For he knew her own Dove,

By the Feathers she wore:
'Till furious Love sallying,
At last he fell dallying,
And down, down he got him,
But oh! oh how sweet, and how soft at the Bottom.

The Shepherdess blushing,
To think what she'd done;
Away from the Shepherd,
She fain wou'd have run;
Which Strephon perceiving,
The wand'rer did seize;
And cry'd do be angry,
Fair Nymph if you please:
'Tis too late to be cruel,
Thy Frowns my dear Jewel,
Now no more Stings have got 'em,
For oh! Thou'rt all kind, and all soft at the Bottom.

THE MOUNTEBANK SONG

[*c.* 1720]

[From *Pills to Purge Melancholy* (1720), v. 311].

See, Sirs, see here! a Doctor rare, who travels much at home!
Here take my Pills, take my Pills,
I cure all Ills,
Past, present, and to come;
The Cramp, the Stitch,
The Squirt, the Itch, the Gout, the Stone,
The Pox, the Mulligrubs, the Bonny Scrubs, and all, all, all, all, all, Pandora's Box: Thousands I've Dissected,
Thousands new erected, and such Cures effected, as none e'er can tell.
Let the Palsie shake ye, let the Chollick rack ye,
Let the Crinkums break ye, let the Murrain take ye;
Take this, take this and you are well.
Thousands I've Dissected, Thousands new erected, and such Cures effected, as none e'er can tell.
Come Wits so keen, devour'd with Spleen;
Come Beaus who sprain'd your Backs,

Great-belly'd Maids,
Old founder'd Jades, and Pepper'd Vizard Cracks.
I soon remove the pains of Love,
And cure the Love-sick Maid;
The Hot, the Cold, the Young, the Old,
The Living and the Dead.
I clear the Lass with Wainscot Face, and from
Pim-ginets free,
Plump Ladies Red, like Saracen's head, with
toaping Rattafe.
This with a Jirk, will do your work,
And scour you o're and o're,
Read, Judge and Try, and if you die,
Never believe me more.
Never, never, never, never, never believe me more.

THE SOLDIERS RETURN FROM THE WARS;

OR

THE MAIDS AND WIDDOWS REJOYCING

[*c.* 1720]

[From *Pills to Purge Melancholy* (1720), vi. 324; music, *ibid.*, p. 278].

At the Change as I was walking,
  I heard a Discourse of Peace;
The People all were a Talking,
  That the tedious Wars will cease:
And if it do prove but true,
The Maids will run out of their Houses,
  To see the Troopers all come Home,
  And the Grenadiers with their Drum a Drum
    Drum,
Then the Widows shall all have Spouses.

The Scarlet colour is fine, Sir,
  All others it doth excel;
The Trooper has a Carbine, Sir,
  That will please the Maidens well:

And when it is Cock'd and Prim'd, Sir,
The Maids will run out of their Houses, &c.

There's Joan, and Betty, and Nelly,
  And the rest of the Female Crew;
Each has an Itch in her Belly,
  To play with the Scarlet hue:
And Marg'ret too must be peeping,
  To see the Troopers all come Home, &c.

The Landladys are preparing,
  Her Maids are shifting their Smocks;
Each swears she'll buy her a Fairing,
  And opens her Christmas-box:
She'll give it all to the Red-coats,
  When as the Troopers all come Home, &c.

Jenny she lov'd a Trooper,
  And she shew'd her all her Gear:
Doll has turn'd off the Cooper,
  And now for a Grenadier:
His hand Grenadoes they will please her,
  When as the Troopers all come Home, &c.

Old musty Maids that have Money,
  Although no Teeth in their Heads;
May have a Bit for their Bunny,
  To pleasure them in their Beds:
Their Hearts will turn to the Red-coats,
  When as the Troopers all come Home, &c.

The Widdows now are a Singing,
  And have thrown their Peaks aside;
For they have been us'd to stinging,
  When their Garters were unty'd:
But the Red-coats they will tye 'em,
  When as the Troopers all come Home, &c.

Wives and Widdows and Maidens,
  I'm sure this News will please ye;
If any with Maiden-heads laden,
  The Red-coats they will ease ye:
Then all prepare to be happy,
  To see the Troopers all come Home, &c.

THE PRESSING CONSTABLE

[*c.* 1720]

[From *Pills to Purge Melancholy* (1720), vi. 236; music set by R. LEVERIDGE].

I am a cunning Constable,
  And a Bag of Warrants I have here,
To press sufficient Men, and able,
  At Horn-castle to appear:
But now-a-days they're grown so cunning,
  That hearing of this Martial strife;
They all away from hence are running,
  Where I miss the Man, I'll press the Wife.

Ho, who'se at Home? Lo, here am I,
  Good-morrow Neighbour. Welcome, Sir;
Where is your Husband? Why truly
  He's gone abroad, a Journey far:
Do you not know when he comes back?
  See how these Cowards fly for Life!
The King for Soldiers must not lack,
  If I miss the Man, I'll take the Wife.

Shew me by what Authority
  You do it? Pray Sir, let me know;

It is sufficient for to see,
  The Warrant hangs in Bag below:
Then pull it out, if it be strong,
  With you I will not stand at strife:
My Warrant is as broad as long,
  If I miss the Man, I'll Press the Wife.

Now you have Prest me and are gone,
  Please you but let me know your Name;
That when my Husband he comes home,
  I may declare to him the same:
My Name is Captain Ward, I say,
  I ne'er fear'd Man in all my life:
The King for Soldiers must not stay,
  Missing the Man, I'll Press the Wife.

BONNY KATHERN LOGGY

[*c.* 1720]

[From *Pills to Purge Melancholy* (1720), vi. 275].

As I came down the hey Land Town,
  There was Lasses many,
Sat in a Rank, on either Bank,
  And ene more gay than any;
Ise leekt about for ene kind Face,
  And Ise spy'd Willy Scroggy;
Ise spir'd of him what was her Name,
  And he caw'd her Kathern Loggy.

A sprightly bonny Gurl sha was,
  And made my Heart to rise Joe;
Sha was so fair sa blith a Lass,
  And Love was in her Eyes so:
Ise walkt about like ene possest,
  And quite forgot poor Moggy;
For nothing now could give me rest,
  But bonny Kathern Loggy.

My pratty Katy then quoth I,
  And many a Sigh I gave her;

Let not a Leard for Katy die,
  But take him to great Favour:
Sha laught aloud, and sa did aw,
  And bad me hemward to ge;
And still cry'd out awaw, awaw,
  Fro bonny Kathern Loggy.

A Fardel father I would see,
  And some began to muse me;
The Lasses they sat wittally,
  And the Lads began to Rooze me:
The Blades with Beaus came down she knows,
  Like ring Rocks fro Strecy Boggy;
And four and twanty Highland Lads,
  Were following Kathern Loggy.

When I did ken this muckle Trame,
  And every ene did know her;
I spir'd of Willy what they mean,
  Quo he they aw do Mow her:
There's ne'er a Lass in aw Scotland,
  From Dundee to Strecy Boggy;
That has her Fort so bravely Mann'd,
  As bonny Kathern Loggy.

At first indeed I needs must tell,
  Ise could not well believe it;
But when Ise saw how fow they fell,
  Ise could not but conceive it.

There was ne'er a Lad of any none,
  Or any deaf young Roguey;
But he did lift the welly Coat,
Of bonny Kathern Loggy.

Had I kenn'd on Kittleness,
  As I came o'er the Moore Joe;
Ise had n'er ban as Ise ha dun,
  Nor e'er out-stankt my seln so:
For I was then so stankt with stint,
  I spurr'd my aw'd Nagg Fogey;
And had I kenn'd sha had been a Whore,
  I had ne'er Lov'd Kathern Loggy.

LUMPS OF PUDDING

[*c.* 1720]

[From *Pills to Purge Melancholy* (1720), vi. 300].

When I was in the low Country,
When I was in the low Country;
What slices of Pudding and pieces of Bread,
My Mother gave me when I was in need.

My Mother she killed a good fat Hog,
She made such Puddings would choak a Dog;
And I shall ne'er forget 'till I dee,
What lumps of Pudding my Mother gave me.

She hung them up upon a Pin,
The Fat run out and the Maggots crept in;
If you won't believe me you may go and see,
What lumps of Pudding my Mother gave me.

And every Day my Mother would cry,
Come stuff your Belly Girl until you die;
Twou'd make you to laugh if you were to see,
What lumps of Pudding my Mother gave me.

I no sooner at Night was got into Bed,
But she all in kindness would come with speed;
She gave me such parcels I thought I should dee,
With eating of Pudding my Mother gave me.

At last I Rambled abroad and then,
I met in my Frolick an honest Man;
Quoth he my dear Philli I'll give unto thee,
Such Pudding you never did see.

Said I honest Man, I thank thee most kind,
And as he told me indeed I did find;
He gave me a lump which did so agree,
One bit was worth all my Mother gave me.

"I'LL PRESS, I'LL BLESS THEE CHARMING FAIR"

[*c.* 1720]

[From *Pills to Purge Melancholy* (1720), vi. 297].

I'll press, I'll bless thee Charming fair,
  Thou Darling of my Heart;
I'll press, I'll bless thee Charming fair,
  Thou darling of my Heart:
I'll clasp, I'll grasp thee close my Dear,
  And Doat on every Part.

I'll clasp, I'll grasp thee close my Dear,
  And Doat on every Part!
I'll bless thee now thou Darling,
  Thou Darling of my Heart;
I'll bless thee now thou Darling,
  Thou Darling of my Heart.

With fond excess of Pleasure,
  I'll make the Panting cry, Panting cry;
Then wisely use your Treasure,
Then wisely use your Treasure,
  Refusing, still comply.

"LAIS WHEN YOU LYE WRAPP'D IN CHARMS"

[*c.* 1720]

[From *Pills to Purge Melancholy* (1720), vi. 295].

Lais when you
Lye wrapp'd in Charms,
In your Spouses Arms,
How can you deny,
The Youth to try,
What is his due.

Sure you ne'er have
Been touch'd by Man,
That you ne'er can,
Admit the Slave.

Come let him in,
And if he does
Not pay what he owes,
Ne'er trust the Fool again.

Let another Spark supply his Place,
For a Woman should not want;

And Nature sure ne'er made a Man so base,
But with asking he would grant:
But if all Mankind were agreed to spoil your Race,
By Jove my Dear they shan't.

PERKIN IN A COLE-SACK;

OR

THE COLLIER'S BUXOME WIFE OF ST. JAMES'S

[*c.* 1720]

[From *Pills to Purge Melancholy* (1720), vi. 255].

Come all that are disposed a while,
  And listen to my Story;
I shall not you of ought beguile,
  But plainly lay before ye:
How Buxome Ruth had often strove,
  With no small Pains and Labour;
Her own Sufficiency to prove,
  By many a Brawny Neighbour.

She oft was heard for to Complain,
  But still with little Profit;
That Nature made her Charms in vain,
  Unless some good come of it:
Her Booby seldom was at home,
  And therefore could not please her;

Which made more welcome Guest to come,
 In Charity to ease her.

Her wishes all were for an Heir,
 Tho' Venus still refus'd her;
Which made the pensive Sinner Swear,
 The Goddess had abus'd her:
And since her Suit she did deny,
 To shew her good Intention;
She was resolv'd her self to try
 An Old, but rare Invention.

Abroad by known Example taught,
 To one with Child she hasts her;
Whereby five Guineas which she brought,
 The Bargain is made fast, Sir:
The Infant soon as brought to light,
 (For so they had agreed it)
Must fall to Buxome Ruth by right,
 To save her sinking Credit.

Her petticoats with Cushions rear'd,
 Her Belly struts before her;
Her Ben's Abilitys are prais'd,
 And he poor Fool adores her.
Her Stomach sick, and squeamish grown,
 She pewkes like Breeding Woman,
While he is proud to make it known,
 That he has prov'd a true Man.

Nine Months compleat, the trusty Dame,
  Her Pain she finds increases;
While Ruth affected with the same,
  Makes ugly and wry Faces:
And now a Coach must needs be had,
  The Brat to shake about, Sir;
But e'er return'd Ben was a Dad,
  For Perkin had crept out, Sir.

The good Ale Firkin strait is tapp'd,
  And Women all are Jolly;
While no one in her round is 'scap'd,
  For fear of Melancholy:
And Ruth in Bed could in her turn,
  Tho' modest of Behaviour;
With all her Heart a Bob have born,
  Had she not fear'd a Feaver.

Thus Jovially the time they spend,
  In Merriment and Quaffing;
Whilst each one does the Brat commend,
  As Ben did still keep Laughing:
And now to tell is my Intent,
  How Fortune to Distaste her;
Ruth's future Boasting did prevent,
  By one most sad Disaster.

A Search was made at t'other Home,
  By Overseers quick sighted;

The Mother to Confession comes,
  By Threats being much Affrighted;
Thus all their Mirth at once was Cool,
  Fate all their hopes did hamper;
So Ben lives on the self same Fool,
  Tho' Ruth was forc'd to scamper.

And if the Truth of this you doubt,
The Overseers can make it out.

THE BONNY LASS;

OR

THE BUTTON'D SMOCK

[*c.* 1720]

From *Pills to Purge Melancholy* (1720), vi. 145].

Sit you merry Gallants,
  For I can tell you News,
Of a Fashion call'd the Button'd Smock,
  The which our Wenches use:
Because that in the City,
  In troth it is great pity;
Our Gallants hold it much in scorn,
  They should put down the City:
But is not this a bouncing Wench,
  And is not this a Bonny;
In troth she wears a Holland Smock,
  If that she weareth any.

A bonny Lass in a Country Town,
  Unto her Commendation;
She scorns a Holland Smock
  Made after the old Fashion:

But she will have it Holland fine,
  As fine as may be wore;
Hem'd and stitch'd with Naples Silk,
  And button'd down before:
But is not this a bouncing Wench, &c.

Our Gallants of the City,
  New Fashions do devise;
And wear such new found fangle things,
  Which country Folk despise:
As for the Button'd Smock,
  None can hold it in scorn;
Nor none can think the Fashion ill,
  It is so closely worn:
Although it may be felt,
  It's seldom to be seen;
It passeth all the Fashions yet,
  That heretofore hath been.
But is not this a bouncing Wench, &c.

Our Wenches of the City,
  That gains the Silver rare;
Sometimes they wear a Canvass Smock,
  That's torn or worn Thread-bare;
Perhaps a Smock of Lockrum,
  That's dirty, foul, or black:
Or else a Smock of Canvass course,
  As hard as any Sack.
But is not this a bouncing Wench, &c.

But she that wears the Holland Smock,
I commend her still that did it;
To wear her under Parts so fine,
The more 'tis for her Credit:
For some will have the out-side fine,
To make the braver show;
But she will have her Holland Smock
That's Button'd down below.
But is not this a bouncing Wench, &c.

But if that I should take in hand,
Her Person to commend;
I should vouchsafe a long Discourse,
The which I could not end:
For her Vertues they are many,
Her person likewise such;
But only in particular,
Some part of them I'll touch.
But is not this a bouncing Wench, &c.

Those Fools that still are doing,
With none but costly Dames;
With tediousness of wooing,
Makes cold their hottest flames:
Give me the Country Lass,
That trips it o'er the Field;
And ope's her Forest at the first,
And is not Coy to yield.
But is not this a bouncing Wench, &c.

Who when she dons her Vesture,
  She makes the Spring her Glass;
And with her Comely gesture,
  Doth all the Meadows pass:
Who knows no other cunning,
  But when she feels it come;
To gripe your Back, if you be slack,
  And thrust your Weapon home.
But is not this a bouncing Wench, &c.

'Tis not their boasting humour,
  Their painted looks nor state;
Nor smells of the Perfumer,
  The Creature doth create:
Shall make me unto these,
  Such slavish service owe;
Give me the Wench that freely takes,
  And freely doth bestow.
But is not this a bouncing Wench, &c.

Who far from all beguiling,
  Doth not her Beauty Mask;
But all the while lye smiling,
  While you are at your task:
Who in the midst of Pleasure,
  Will beyond active strain;
And for your Pranks, will con you thanks,
  And curtsey for your pain.
But is not this a bouncing Wench, &c.

THE HUNT

[*c.* 1720]

[From *Pills to Purge Melancholy* (1720), vi. 127].

Some in the Town go betimes to the Downs,
  To pursue the fearful Hare;
Some in the Dark love to hunt in a Park,
  For to chace all the Deer that are there:
Some love to see the Faulcon to flee,
  With a joyful rise against the Air;
But all my delight is a Cunny in the Night,
  When she turns up her silver Hair.

When she is beset, with a Bow, Gun, or Net,
  And finding no shelter for to cover her;
She falls down flat, or in a Tuft does squat,
  'Till she lets the Hunter get over her:
With her breast she does butt, and she bubs up
    her Scut,
  When the Bullets fly close by her Ear;
She strives not to escape, but she mumps like
    an Ape,
  And she turns up her silver Hair.

The Ferret he goes in, through flaggs thick
and thin,
Whilst Mettle pursueth his Chace;
The Cunny she shows play, and in the best of
her way,
Like a Cat she does spit in his Face:
Tho' she lies in the Dust, she fears not his Nest,
With her full bound up Sir, career;
With the strength that she shows, she gapes at
the Nose,
And she turns up her silver Hair.

The sport is so good, that in Town or in Wood,
In a Hedge, or a Ditch you may do it;
In Kitchen or in Hall, in a Barn or in a Stall,
Or wherever you please you may go to it:
So pleasing it is that you can hardly miss,
Of so rich Game in all our Shire;
For they love so to play, that by Night or by
Day,
They will turn up their Silver Hair.

THE TRAVELLING TINKER, AND THE COUNTRY ALE-WIFE;

OR

THE LUCKY MENDING OF THE LEAKY COPPER

[*c.* 1720]

[From *Pills to Purge Melancholy* (1720), vi. 296].

A Comely Dame of Islington,
  Had got a leaky Copper;
The Hole that let the Liquor run,
  Was wanting of a Stopper:
A Jolly Tinker undertook,
  And promised her most fairly;
With a thump thump thump, and knick knack knock,
  To do her Business rarely.

He turn'd the Vessel to the Ground,
  Says he a good old Copper;
But well may't Leak, for I have found
  A Hole in't that's a whopper:
But never doubt a Tinkers stroke,
  Altho' he's black and surly,

With a thump thump thump, and knick knack
knock,
He'll do your Business purely.

The Man of Mettle open'd wide,
His Budget's mouth to please her,
Says he this Tool we oft employ'd,
About such Jobbs as these are:
With that the Jolly Tinker took,
A Stroke or two most kindly;
With a thump thump thump, and knick knack
knock,
He did her Business finely.

As soon as Crock had done the Feat,
He cry'd 'tis very hot ho;
This thrifty Labour makes me Sweat,
Here, gi's a cooling Pot ho:
Says she bestow the other Stroke,
Before you take your Farewel;
With a thump thump thump, and knick knack
knock,
And you may drink a Barrel.

A TOPING SONG

[*c.* 1720]

[From *Pills to Purge Melancholy* (1720), vi. 200].

I am a Jolly Toper, I am a raged Soph,
Known by the Pimples in my Face, with taking
Bumpers off,
And a Toping we will go, we'll go, we'll go,
And a Toping we will go.

Come let's sit down together, and take our fill
of Beer,
Away with all disputes, for we'll have no
Wrangling her,
And a Toping we will go, &c.

With clouds of Tobacco we'll make our Noddles
clear,
We'll be as great as Princes, when our Heads
are full of Beer,
And a Toping we will go, &c.

With Juggs, Muggs, and Pitchers, and Bellarmines
of Stale,

Dash'd lightly with a little, a very little Ale,
And a Toping we will go, &c.

A Fig for the Spaniard, and for the King of France,
And Heaven preserve our Juggs, and Muggs, and Q—n from all mischance,
And a Toping we will go, &c.

Against the Presbyterians, pray give me leave to rail,
Who ne'er had thirsted for Kings Blood, had they been Drunk with stale,
And a Toping we will go, &c.

And against the Low-church Saints, who slily play their part,
Who rail at the Dissenters, yet love them in their Heart,
And a Toping we will go, &c.

Here's a Health to the Queen, let's Bumpers take in hand,
And may Prince G—'s Roger grow stiff gaing and stand,
And a Toping we will go, &c.

Oh how we toss about the never-failing Cann,
We drink and piss, and piss and drink, and drink to piss again,
And a Toping we will go, &c.

Oh that my Belly it were a Tun of stall,
My Cock were turn'd into a Tap, to run when
I did call,
And a Toping we will go, &c.

Of all sorts of Topers, a Soph is far the best,
For 'till he can neither go nor stand, by Jove
he's ne'er at rest,
And a Toping we will go, &c.

We fear no Wind or Weather, when good Liquor
dwells within,
And since a Soph does live so well, then who
would be a King,
And a Toping we will go, &c.

Then dead Drunk We'll march Boys, and reel
into our Tombs,
That Jollier Sophs (if such their be) may come
and take our rooms.
And a Toping may they go, &c.
And a Toping may they go, may they go, may
they go.
And a Toping may they go.

CLARINDA'S COMPLAINT

[*c.* 1720]

[From *Pills to Purge Melancholy* (1720), vi. 271].

With sighing and wishing, and Green-sickness
Diet,
With nothing of Pleasure, and little of Quiet;
With a Granum's Inspection, and Doctor's
Direction,
But not the Specifick, that suits my Complexion:
The Flower of my Age is full blown in my Face,
Yet no Man considers, yet no Man considers
My comfortless Case.

Young Women were valued, as I have been told,
In the late times of Peace, above Mountains of
Gold;
But now there is Fighting, we are nothing but
sliting,
Few Gallants in Conjugal Matters delighting:
'Tis a shame that Mankind, should love killing
and slaying
And mind not supplying the stock that's decaying.

Unlucky Clarinda, to love in a Season,
When Mars has forgotten to do Venus Reason;
Had I any Hand in Rule and Command,
I'd certainly make it a Law of the Land:
That killers of Men, to replenish the Store,
Be bound to the Wedlock, and made to get more.

Enacted moreover for better dispatch,
That where a good Captain meets with an o'ermatch,
His honest Lieutenant with Soldier-like Grace,
Shall relieve him on Duty, and serve in his Place:
Thus killers and slayers of able good Men,
Without beat of Drum may recruit 'em agen.

THE JOLLY TRADES-MEN

[*c.* 1720]

[From *Pills to Purge Melancholy* (1720), vi. 91].

Sometimes I am a Tapster new,
And skilful in my Trade Sir,
I fill my Pots most duly,
Without deceit or froth Sir:
A Spicket of two Handfuls long,
I use to Occupy Sir:
And when I set a Butt abroach,
Then shall no Beer run by Sir.

Sometimes I am a Butcher,
And then I feel fat Ware Sir;
And if the Flank be fleshed well,
I take no farther care Sir:
But in I thrust my Slaughtering-Knife,
Up to the Haft with speed Sir;
For all that ever I can do,
I cannot make it bleed Sir.

Sometimes I am a Baker,
And Bake both white and brown Sir;
I have as fine a Wrigling-Pole,
As any is in all this Town Sir:

But if my Oven be over-hot,
I dare not thrust in it Sir;
For burning of my Wrigling-Pole,
My Skill's not worth a Pin Sir.

Sometimes I am a Glover,
And can do passing well Sir;
In dressing of a Doe-skin,
I know I do excel Sir:
But if by chance a Flaw I find,
In dressing of the Leather;
I straightway whip my Needle out,
And I tack 'em close together.

Sometimes I am a Cook,
And in Fleet-Street I do dwell Sir:
At the sign of the Sugar-loaf,
As it is known full well Sir:
And if a dainty Lass comes by,
And wants a dainty bit Sir;
I take four Quarters in my Arms,
And put them on my Spit Sir.

In Weavering and in Fulling,
I have such passing Skill Sir;
And underneath my Weavering-Beam,
There stands a Fulling-Mill Sir:
To have good Wives displeasure,
I would be very loath Sir;

The Water runs so near my Hand,
It over-thicks my Cloath Sir.

Sometimes I am a Shoe-maker,
And work with silly Bones Sir;
To make my Leather soft and moist,
I use a pair of Stones Sir:
My Lasts for and my lasting Sticks,
Are fit for every size Sir;
I know the length of Lasses Feet,
By handling of their Thighs Sir.

The Tanner's Trade I practice,
Sometimes amongst the rest Sir;
Yet I could never get a Hair,
Of any Hide I dress'd Sir;
For I have been tanning of a Hide,
This long seven Years and more Sir;
And yet it is as hairy still,
As ever it was before Sir.

Sometimes I am a Taylor,
And work with Thread that's strong Sir;
I have a fine great Needle,
About two handfulls long Sir;
The finest Sempster in this Town,
That works by line or leisure;
May use my Needle at a pinch,
And do themselves great Pleasure.

THE BASHFUL LOVER

[*c.* 1729]

[Words by Mr. THEOBALD, from *The Lady's Triumph*].

On a Bank of Flow'rs in a Summer's Day,
  Inviting and undrest,
In her Bloom of Years bright *Celia* lay,
  With Love and Sleep oppres't;
When a youthful Swain with admiring Eyes
Wish'd he durst the fair Maid surprize,
With a *Fa*, *la*, *la*, &c.
  But fear'd approaching Spies.

As he gaz'd, a gentle Breeze arose,
  That fann'd her Robes aside;
And the sleeping Nymph did the Charms disclose,
  Which, waking, She wou'd hide,
Then his Breath grew short, and his Pulse beat high,
He long'd to touch what he chanc'd to spy;
With a *fa*, *la*, *la*, &c.

All amaz'd he stood, with her Beauties fir'd
  And blest the courteous Wind;

Then in Wispers sigh'd, and the Gods desir'd,
  That *Celia* might be kind,
Then with Hope grown bold, he advanc'd amain;
But she laugh'd loud in a Dream, and, again,
With a *fa*, *la*, *la*, &c.
  Repell'd the tim'rous Swain.

Yet when once Desire has inflam'd the Soul,
  All modest Doubts withdraw;
And the God of Love does each Fear controul,
  That wou'd the Lover awe.
Shall a Prize like this, says the vent'rous Boy,
'Scape, and I not the Means employ,
With a *fa*, *la*, *la*, &c.
  To seize the proffer'd Toy?

Here the glowing Youth, to relieve his Pain,
  The slumb'ring Maid caress'd;
And with trembling Hands (O the simple Swain!)
  Her glowing Bosom press'd:
When the Virgin wak'd, and affrighted flew,
Yet look'd, as wishing he wou'd pursue,
With a *fa*, *la*, *la*, &c.
  But *Damon* miss'd his Cue.

Now, repenting that he had let her fly,
  Himself he thus accus'd;
What a dull and stupid Thing was I
  That such a chance abus'd?

To my Shame 'twill now on the Plains be said,
Damon a Virgin asleep betray'd,
With a *fa*, *la*, *la*, &c.
  Yet let her go a Maid.

THE DYER OF ROAN

[*c.* 1729]

[From *Musical Miscellany* (1729), iii. 60; tune, *Old Simon the King*].

In good King Lewis's Land,
  In a City of high Degree,
There liv'd a Dyer grand,
  And a very good Dyer was he.
This Dyer was married, forsooth,
  And married in Truth was he,
To a Maid in the Bloom of her Youth;
  And she gave him some Jea-lou-sy.

In vain had he sought to discover,
  What he little desir'd to see,
Never dreaming his Wife had a Lover
  Of Monkey-fac'd Monsieur *l'Abbée.*
He thought of a politick way,
  To bring all the Matter to light,
By his feigning a Journey one Day,
  And by lying in Ambush at Night.

The Horses were brought to the Door,
  Ev'ry Sign of a Journey appears,

Whilst his Wife (that dissembling Whore)
Was bedew'd in her Crocodile-Tears.
A thousand Grimaces she made,
To shew forth her Grief at his Parting;
But that was the Trick of the Jade,
And regardless as old Women's Farting.

The Dyer was now out of Sight
And prepar'd to discover the Treason;
You will find he was much in the right,
And I'm going to tell you the Reason:
The Wife was no sooner alone,
But she sent for her Father-Confessor:
He put his best Pantaloons on,
And he ran like the Devil to bless her.

The Damsel with Smiles on her Face,
Met the Abbot, and gave him a Kiss;
But no man would have been in his Place,
If he had known of the Jerquer in Piss.
We now may suppose them together
Confessing and Pressing each other;
Bound fast, in Love's Thong of Whit-leather,
Was the Reverend Catholick Brother.

Some Hours were past at this Rate
When the Husband, with *pass-par-tout* Keys,
Made no Scruple to open his Gate,
And caught napping the Hog in his Pease.

Father Abbot, quoth he (without Passion)
  Is this your Church-way of Confession?
Altho' tis a Thing much in Fashion,
  It is nevertheless a Transgression.

The Abbot, as you may believe,
  Had but little to say for himself;
He knew well what he ought to receive,
  For his being so arrant an Elf;
His Cloaths he got on with all Speed,
  And conducted he was by the Dyer,
To be duckt (as you after may read)
  And be cool'd from his amorous Fire.

Quoth the Dyer, Most Reverend Father,
  Since I find you're so hot upon Wenching,
I have gather'd my Servants together,
  To give you a Taste of our Drenching.
Here . . . *Tom, Harry, Roger* and *Dick!*
  Take the Abbot, undress him, and douse him;
They obey'd in that very same Nick,
  To the Dye-Vat they take him, and souse him.

To behold what a Figure he made,
  Such a Monster there never was seen;
'Twas enough to make *Satan* afraid;
  He was colour'd all over with Green.
The Dyer had Pleasure enough,
  When he thought how he dy'd him for Life;

'Twas much better than using him rough,
  Since he only had lain with his Wife.

The Abbot was led to the Door,
  And he took to his Heels in a Trice,
Never looking behind or before;
  It was now not a time to be nice.
'Tis reported by some of his Neighbours,
  That he did not discover 'till Morning
The excellent Fruits of his Labours,
  Nor the Colour he had for his Horning.

But, good lack, when he came to the Glass,
  And beheld such a strange Alteration,
He was dy'd of the Colour of Grass,
  And had like to have dy'd with Vexation.
As this Stain can be never got out,
  And the Abbot must lose the Church-Fleece
Let him bear the Disgrace (like a Lout)
  To be shewn for a Penny a piece.

"YOU FAIR, WHO PLAY TRICKS"

VERSES UPON A MISTAKE THAT HAPPENED IN ADMINISTRING A CLYSTER TO A LADY AT WINDSOR

[*c.* 1731]

[From *Windsor Medley*, p. 13; tune, *Hey-derry-down*].

You Fair, who play Tricks to be fairer, draw near,
As a Warning to tamper no more you shall hear,
What a prank of this kind had one like to have cost,
And the best in all Christendom had like to have lost. *Derry-down.*

All know what is good to assist the Digestion,
To clear Poets Brains, and a Lady's Complexion;
To name it out-right, I've been told 'tis not clean,
And none are so dull not to know what I mean.

A Nymph who ne'er yet work'd in Hymen's soft Yoke,

To heighten her Charms, once this Med'cine
bespoke;
She's Chaste as she's Fair, and a Virgin of
Honour,
Who lawfully wishes to take Man upon her.

None hold it absurd, that to brighten her Face
She should think of applying a Wash to her A—e;
If a fair Flower droops, to enliven the Shoot,
You touch not the Top, but you water the Root.

The Things were all ready, the Nymph on
her Bed,
Her B— lay exalted, and low lay her Head;
Her Coats o'er her Neck were conveniently thrown,
And I wou'd, but I dare not, tell all that was
shown.

The Maid now approaches to begin Operation,
No Monarch, I ween, but might covet the Station;
Laud! what are you fumbling; she cry'd, *Betty*
come,
If you follow your Nose, you're as sure as a Gun.

With your Hand try the Heat tho' before you
begin,
And for G—'s sake take care to grease well the
Machine;

For your Thing is so stiff, and my Hole is so small,
If you enter too roughly, I surely shall squall.

Never doubt of my Caution, poor *Betty* reply'd,
But lend your Hand, my dear Miss, and that shall be my Guide;
Miss lent her her Hand, and Miss gave her her Cue,
But her Business, alas! *Betty's* Thing wou'd not do.

It was thrust in as far as 'twou'd go, but in vain,
Miss cry'd, I feel nothing, good *Betty*, but Pain;
And such Pain, that not more I believe 'twould have cost,
Were a Man on the Bed, and my Maiden-head lost.

Let us open the Bladder—the Devil, what's here?
I smell Vinegar sure—Is this, *Betty*, your care?
Pray see all the Liquor is turn'd to a Curd,
'Tis no wonder your Clyster dont prove worth a T—d.

How the old Proverb lyes, that says, Sh—n Luck's good!

Had I taken the Medicine, 't had surely fetch'd
Blood;
Nay, so sharp is its Nature, if once that comes
there,
I believe it had flea'd me all around to a Hair.

When Danger was near, one thanks G— for
the 'Scape,
I could not ha' been gladder had it been from
a Rape.
Then I'll try no more Tricks, but let Nature
prevail,
For it shan't be a Maid that pokes next in my
T—l.

So she drest, and away to the Circle at C—t,
The Brightest of all, where the Brightest resort;
Nor wanted to borrow Assistance from Art,
To delight every Eye, and attack every Heart.

THE PENITENT NUN

[*c.* 1731]

[By JOHN LOCKMAN; from *Musical Miscellany* (1731), vi. 184; set by MR. HAYM].

Dame *Jane* a sprightly Nun, and gay,
  And form'd of very yielding Clay,
Had long with resolution strove
  To guard against the Shafts of Love.
Fond *Cupid* smiling, spies the Fair,
  And soon he baffles all her Care,
In vain she tries her Pain to smother,
  The Nymph too frail, the Nymph too frail,
      becomes a Mother.

But no, these little Follies o'er,
  She firmly vows she'll sin no more;
No more to Vice will fall a Prey,
  But spend in Prayer each fleeting Day.
Close in her Cell immur'd she lies,
  Nor from the Cross removes her Eyes;
Whilst Sisters crouding at the Crate,
  Spend all their Time, spend all their Time in
      Worldly Prate.

The Abbess, overjoy'd to find
  This happy Change in Jenny's Mind,
The rest, with Air compos'd, addressing,
  "Daughters, if you expect a Blessing,
"From pious *Jane*, Example take,
  "The World and all its Joys forsake."
"We will (they all reply'd as One)
  "But first let's do as *Jane* has done."

FANCY'S ALL;

OR

JOAN AS GOOD AS MY LADY

[*c.* 1731]

[Words by Mr. MITCHELL; from *Musical Miscellany* (1731), vi. 132; tune, *Lesly's March*, by DAVID RIZZIO].

Black, *White*, *Yellow* or *Red*,
Woman's a charming lovely Creature
Get her but fairly to *Bed*
And boggle no more about the Matter,
Tis not *Complexion*,
That causes *Affection*;
Nor *Graces* appearing,
That make her endearing;
But *Fancy* in *Lovers*,
Such secrets discovers
As presently set their Spirits in motion.
Woman's a Treasure,
Created for *Pleasure;*
And what are their *Faces*,
Compar'd to *Embraces?*
If *Joan* is but ready,
She's good as her *Lady*:
A Proof that *Delight* is the Daughter of *Notion*.

"MY JOCKY BLYTH FOR WHAT THOU HAST DONE"

[*c.* 1733]

[From *Orpheus Caledonius*, ii. 88; tune, *Come kiss with me, come clap with me*].

PEGGY

My *Jocky* blyth for what thou hast done,
  There is nae help nor mending;
For thou hast jogg'd me out of Tune,
  For a' thy fair pretending.
My Mither sees a Change on me,
  For my Complexion dashes,
And this alas! has been with thee
  Sae late amang the Rashes.

JOCKY

My *Peggy*, what I've said I'll do,
  To free thee frae her Scouling;
Come then, and let us buckle to,
  Nae langer let's be fooling:
For her content I'll instant wed,
  Since thy Complexion dashes;

And then we'll try a Feather-bed,
  'Tis faster than the Rashes.

PEGGY

Then *Jocky* since thy Love's so true,
  Let Mither scoul, I'm easy:
Sae lang's I live I ne'er shall rue
  For what I've done to please thee.
And there's my hand I'le ne'er complain:
  O! well's me on the Rashes;
When e'er thou likes I'll do't again
  And a Feg for a' their Clashes.

THE WAY TO WIN HER

[*c.* 1766]

[From *The Rattle*, by DURFEY THE YOUNGER, p. 55; tune, *The Way to keep him*].

Ye Swains who roam from fair to fair,
And strive each heart to bind,
Give ear to what I now declare
The precepts of a friend.
Would you in *Venus* wars succeed,
Of bashfulness be sure take heed,
And that's the Way to Win her.

When first you meet the blooming lass,
More ripe than peach or pear,
Let not the minutes idly pass,
Of dull delays beware:
With kisses sweet your flame confess,
Her panting snowy bosom press,
And that's the Way to Win her.

But should the crafty nymph prove coy,
Cry "Fye, Sir, you are rude,"
Let not those arts you[r] hopes destroy,

By nature all are lewd.
Then shilly shally never stand,
But boldly march up sword in hand
And that's the Way to Win her.

And when *love's* fire you have fann'd,
And she begins to melt,
And finds her virtue can't withstand
The raptures she has felt;
Then gently force her to the sport
With resolution storm the fort,
And that's the Way to Win her.

NOBODY AND NOTHING

[1772]

[From *Songs Comic and Satyrical*, by G. A. STEVENS (1772), 237; tune, *Gee-ho Dobbin*].

A story or song, you have left to my choice,
For one I've no humour, for t'other no voice;
In attempting a tune I like *Nobody* bawl,
And as to a mimic I'm *Nothing* at all.

The wrinkl'd-cheek Critic, call'd *'Squire Syntaxis*,
Pedantical speaking, wou'd bring into practice,
With classical gabble may wink and may sneer,
And beg I wou'd make the thing *Nothing* appear.

For schoolmasters congregate derivate stuff,
I speak to be understood, that is enough;
The phrase of like *Nobody* they may condemn,
But as I sing *Nothing*, 'tis *Nothing* to them.

Now as to this *Nobody* I dare to say,
Altho' we see *Somebody* always in play;
And *sometimes* that *something* may *somehow* be
shewn,
Yet *Nobody* only must *many things* own.

The public is pester'd with many gay forms,
Like butterflies, springing from grubs and from
worms;
Those *well-dress'd necessities* daily we view,
In *Nobody's* business with *Nothing* to do.

They've *Nothing* to think on, they've *Nothing* to
say,
Nobody's all night, and just *Nothing* all day;
At *Nothing* they laugh, and at *Nothing* they cry,
And *Nobody* cares how they live or they dye.

'Tis *Nobody* only can guess the game play'd,
When *Nobody's* by, betwixt master and maid;
Unless Indiscretion shou'd alter their plan,
Nobody knows *Nothing* 'twixt mistress and man.

The romp too ripe grown, unless gathr'd a spouse,
Will fall, the first shake, from weak Chastity's
boughs;
Dear Captain, she whispers, *somebody* will hear us,
Dear Miss, whispers he, there is *Nobody* near us.

But when she's betray'd by her passion, to shame,
And parents and guardians begin with their blame;
Who, *I Sir?—not I, Sir!—no! Honour forbid it,
If I am with Child, it was* NOBODY *did it.*

The tread of Gallant by Cornuto is heard,
On tiptoe the lover from rendezvous scar'd;

Who's there? starts the husband, *'tis thieves that
I hear*,
But wife pats his cheek, and lisps, *Nobody!* dear.

Any-body may say, if they please, I am wrong,
Every-body find fault, if they please, with my song;
But careful lest *Somebody* we shou'd offend,
I with *Nothing* began, and with *Nobody* end.

CHASTITY

[1772]

[From *Songs Comic and Satyrical*, by G. A. STEVENS (1772), 159; tune, *Good people I'll tell you no Rhodamontade*].

I wonder, quoth Dame, as her Spouse she embraces,
How strumpets can look, how they dare shew their faces,
And those wicked Wives who from Husband's arms fly
Lord, where do they think they must go when they die?

But next day, by Husband, with 'Prentice Boy caught,
When she from the bed was to Toilet-glass brought,
Her head he held up, with this gentle Rebuke—
My Dear! you was wishing to know how Whores look!

Turn your eyes to that table, at once you will see
What faces Jades wear; then, my Dear, behold *me*
Your Features confess the Adultress clear,
My visage exhibits how Cuckolds appear.

You ask'd where bad Wives go? why, really, my
Chick,
You must with the rest of them go to *Old Nick!*
If *Belzebub* don't such damn'd Tennants disown
For bad Wives, he knows make a Hell of their own.

All the world wou'd be wed, if the Clergy could shew
Any rule in the service to change *I* for *O:*
How happy the Union of Marriage wou'd prove,
Not long as we *Live* join'd, but long as we *Love.*

At his feet she sunk down, Sorrow let her such
Moans
That Resentment was gagg'd by her Tears and
her Tones.
What cou'd *Hubby* do then? what cou'd then
Hubby do?
But Sympathy struck, as she cry'd, he cry'd too.

O *Corregio!* cou'd I *Sigismunda* design
Or exhibit a *Magdalen, Guido,* like thine,
I wou'd paint the fond Look which the Penitent
stole,
That pierced her soft Partner, and sunk to his Soul.

Transported to doating! he rais'd the Distress'd,
And tenderly held her long time to his Breast;
On the Bed gently laid her, by her gently laid,
And the Breach there was clos'd the same way it
was made.

DICK AND DOLL

[*c.* 1782]

[From *Convivial Songster* (1782), 80; tune, *I'm like a skiff on the ocean toss'd*].

As one bright summer's sultry day,
  For sake of shade I sought the grove
Thro' thickset-hedge, on top of hay,
  I met with mutual love.
A youth with one arm round his pretty girl's waist,
On small swelling-breasts he his other hand plac'd,
    While she cry'd, Dick be still,
    Pray tell me what's your will?

"I come (quoth Dick) to have some chat,"
  And close to hers his lips he squeez'd;
"I guess (cries Doll) what you'd be at,
  "But now I won't be teaz'd."
She strove to rise up, but his strength held her down,
She call'd out for help! and petitioned the clown,
    "O Dick—O dear—lie still!
    "You shall not have your will.

"I'll tear your soul out!—Lord these men!—
  "If ever—well—I wont submit.

"Why?—what? she devil!—Curse me then!—
"You'll fling me in a fit!"
Down, like a bent lily, her head dropp'd aslant;
Her eyes lost the day-light, her breath became scant,
And feebly on her tongue
Expiring accents hung.

The chorus birds sang o'er their heads;
The breeze blew rustling thro' the grove;
Sweet smelt the hay, on new-mown meads:
All seem'd the scene of love.
Dick offer'd to lift up the lass as she lay;
A look, full of tenderness told him to stay.
"So soon, Dick, will you go?
"I wish—dear me!—heigh ho!"

Vibrating with heart-heaving sighs,
Her tucker trembling to and fro',
Her crimson'd cheeks, her glist'ning eyes,
Proclaim'd possession's glow.
Dick bid her farewell; but she lovingly cry'd,
As wanton she play'd by her fallen shepherd's side;
"A moment, pray sit still,
"Since now you've had your will."

"Lord! (cries the girl) you hasty men,
"Of love afford but one poor proof;
"Our fowls at home, each sparrow-hen,

"Are ten times better off."
Dick knew by her languishing what Dolly meant;
Once more view'd her beauties, and soon took
the hint:
Her wishes to fulfil,
He let her have her will.

ACT SEDERUNT O' THE COURT O' SESSION

[1793]

[Original sent by BURNS to ROBT CLEGHORN (1793); from *The Merry Muses of Caledonia* (*c.* 1800); tune, *O'er the muir amang the heather*].

In Embrugh town they've made a law,
In Embrugh, at the Court o' Session,
That stanin' pricks are fau'tors a',
An' guilty o' a high transgression.
Decreet o' the Court o' Session,
Act sederunt o' the Session,
That stanin' pricks are fau'tors a',
An' guilty o' a high transgression.

An' they've provided dungeons deep,
Ilk lass has ane in her possession;
Until the fau'tors wail an' weep,
They there shall lie for their transgression.
Decreet o' the Court o' Session,
Act sederunt o' the Session,
The rogues in pouring tears shall weep,
By act sederunt o' the Session.

GODLY GIRZIE

[*b.* 1796]

[By BURNS; from *The Merry Muses of Caledonia* (*c.* 1800); tune, *Wat ye wha I met yestreen*].

The night it was a holy night,
  The day had been a holy day;
Kilmarnock gleam'd wi' candle light,
  As Girzie hameward took her way.
A man o' sin, ill may he thrive!
  And never holy meeting see!
With godly Girzie met belyve,
  Amang the Craigie hills sae hie.

The chiel' was wight, the chiel' was stark,
  He wad na wait to chap nor ca',
And she was faint wi' holy wark,
  She had na pith to say him na.
But ay she glowr'd up to the moon,
  And ay she sigh'd most piouslie,
"I trust my heart's in heaven aboon,
  "Whare'er your sinfu' pintle be."

COME COW ME MINNIE

[*b.* 1796]

[By BURNS; from *The Merry Muses of Caledonia* (*c.* 1800); tune, *My mither's ay glowrin' at me*].

When Mary cam o'er the border,
When Mary cam o'er the border,
In troth 'twas approachin' the cunt of a hurchin,
Her arse was in sic a disorder.
Come cow me, minnie, come cow me,
Come cow me, minnie, come cow me,
The hair o' my arse is grown into my cunt,
An' they canna win in for to mow me.

But wanton Wattie cam west on't,
But wanton Wattie cam west on't,
He did it sae tickle, he left nae as meikle
As a spider wad biggit a nest on't.
Come cow me, minnie, come cow me, &c.

An' was nae Wattie a blinker?
He mow'd frae the queen to the tinkler;
Then sat down in grief, like the Macedon chief,
For want o' mae warlds to conquer.
Come cow me, minnie, come cow me, &c.

But oh! what a jewel was Mary!
  An' what a jewel was Mary!
Her face it was fine, an' her bosom divine,
  An' her cunt it was theeket wi' glory.
    Come cow me, minnie, come cow me, &c.

THE CASE OF CONSCIENCE

[*b.* 1796]

[By BURNS; from *The Merry Muses of Caledonia* (*c.* 1800); tune, *Auld Sir Symon the King*].

I'll tell you a tale of a wife,
And she was a whig and a saunt;
She liv'd a most sanctified life,
But whyles she was fash'd wi' her cunt.

Poor woman, she gaed to the priest,
And to him she made her complaint,
"There's naething thare troubles my breast,
"Sae sair as the sins o' my cunt."

He bade her to clear up her brow,
And no be discourag'd upon't,
"For holy gude women enow,
"Are mony times waur'd wi' their cunt.

"It's nocht but Beelzebub's art,
"And that's the mair sign o' a saunt;
"He kens that ye're pure at the heart,
"So he levels his darts at your cunt.

"O you that are callèd and free,
"Elskit and chosen a saunt,
"Wilt break the eternal decree,
"Whatever ye do wi' your cunt.

"And now, with a sanctified kiss,
"Let's kneel and renew the cov'nant;
"It's this *** and it's this *** and it's this ***
"That settles the pride of your cunt."

Devotion blew up to a flame,
Nae words can do justice upon't;
The honest auld carlin gaed hame,
Rejoicin' and clawin' her cunt.

Then high to her memory charge,
And may he wha taks it affront;
Still ride in love's channel at large,
But never mak port in a cunt.

YON, YON, YON, LASSIE

[*b.* 1796]

[An old Scots countryside song; from *The Merry Muses of Caledonia* (*c.* 1800), collected by BURNS; tune, *Ruffian's rant;* or, *Cameron's got his wife again*].

I never saw a silken gown,
  But I wad kiss the sleeve o't;
I never met a maidenhead,
  But I wad speir the leave o't.
    O yon, yon, yon, lassie,
      Yon, yon, yon;
    I never met a bonie lass
      But what wad play at yon.

Tell nae me o' Meg my wife
  That crowdie has na flavour;
But gie to me a bonie lass
  An' let me steal the favour.
    O yon, yon, yon, lassie, &c.

Gie me her I kis't yestreen,
  I vow but she was handsome,
For ilka birss upon her cunt
  Was worth a royal ransom.
    O yon, yon, yon, lassie, &c.

AS I LOOK'D O'ER YON CASTLE WA'

[*b.* 1796]

[An old Scots countryside song; from *The Merry Muses of Caledonia* (*c.* 1800), collected by BURNS who transcribed it verbatim in one of his letters to George Thomson].

As I look'd o'er yon castle wa',
  I spied a gray goose an' a gled;
They had a feight between them twa,
  An' O! as their twa hurdies gaed.
    Wi' a hey ding it in, an' a how ding it in,
      An' a hey ding it in, it's lang to-day,
        Fal lary tele, tale, lary tale,
          Fal lary tal, lal lary tay.

She heav'd up, and he strack down,
  Between them twa they made a mow;
That ilka fart that the carlin gae,
  It's four o' them wad fill'd a bowe.
        Wi' a hey ding it in, &c.

"Temper your tail," the carl cried,
  "Temper your tail by Venus' law;"
"Gird hame your gear, gudeman," she cried,
  "Wha the deil can hinder the wind to blaw?"
        Wi' a hey ding it in, &c.

"For were ye on my saddle set,
"An' were ye weel girt in my gear,
"Gin the wind o' my arse blow ye out o' my cunt,
"Ye'll never be reckon'd a man of weir."
Wi' a hey ding it in, &c.

He plac'd his Jacob whare she did piss,
An' his balls where the wind did blaw,
An' he grippit her fast by the gushet o' her arse,
An' he gae her cunt the common law.
Wi' a hey ding it in, &c.

THE COOPER O' CUDDY

[*b.* 1796]

[By Burns; from *The Merry Muses of Caledonia* (*c.* 1800); tune, *Bab at the bowster*].

The cooper o' Cuddy cam here awa',
He ca'd the girrs out o'er us a',
An' our gudewife has gotten a fa',
That anger'd the silly gudeman, O.
We'll hide the cooper behind the door,
Behind the door, behind the door,
We'll hide the cooper behind the door,
For fear o' the auld gudeman, O.

He fought them out, he fought them in,
Wi' deil hae her, an' deil hae him;
But the bodie he was sae doited an' blin',
He wist na whare he was gaun, O.
We'll hide the cooper behind the door, &c.

They cooper'd at e'en, they cooper'd at morn,
Till our gudeman has gotten the scorn;
On ilka brow she's planted a horn,
An' swears that there they shall stan', O.
We'll hide the cooper behind the door, &c.

ANDREW AN' HIS CUTTY GUN

[*b.* 1796]

[An old Scots countryside song; from *The Merry Muses of Caledonia* (*c.* 1800), collected by BURNS].

When a' the lave gaed to their bed,
  And I sat up to clean the shoon,
O, wha think ye cam jumpin' ben
  But Andrew an' his cutty gun?
    Blythe, blythe, blythe was she,
      Blythe was she but and ben;
    An' weel she lo'ed it in her nieve,
      But better when it slippit in.

Or e'er I wish, he laid me back,
  And up my gamon to my chin;
And ne'er a word to me he spak,
  But liltit out his cutty gun.
    Blythe, blythe, blythe was she, &c.

The bawsent bitch she left the whalps,
  And hunted round us at the fun,
As Andrew fodgel'd wi' his arse,

And fir'd at me the cutty gun.
Blythe, blythe, blythe was she, &c.

O, some delight in cutty stoup,
And some delight in cutty-mun
But my delight's an arselins coup
Wi' Andrew and his cutty gun.
Blythe, blythe, blythe was she, &c.

THE YELLOW, YELLOW YORLIN'

[*b.* 1796]

[An old Scots countryside song: from *The Merry Muses of Caledonia* (*c.* 1800), collected by BURNS; tune, *Bonnie beds of roses*; or, *The Collier Laddie*].

It fell on a day, in the flow'ry month o' May,
All on a merry, merry mornin',
I met a pretty maid, an' unto her I said,
"I wad fain fin' your yellow, yellow yorlin'."

"O no, young man", says she, "you're a stranger to me,
"An' I am anither man's darlin',
"Wha has baith sheep an' cows, that's feedin' in the hows,
"An' a cock for my yellow, yellow yorlin'."

"But, if I lay you down upon the dewy ground,
"You wad na be the waur ae farthin',
"An' that happy, happy man, he never cou'd ken
"That I play'd wi' your yellow, yellow yorlin'."

"O fie, young man," says she, "I pray you let me be,
"I wad na for five pounds sterling;
"My mither wad gae mad, an' sae wad my dad,
"If you play'd with my yellow, yellow yorlin'."

But I took her by the waist, an' laid her down in haste,
For a' her squeakin' an' squallin',
The lassie soon grew tame, an' bade me come again
For to play wi' her yellow, yellow yorlin'.

THE FORNICATOR

[*b.* 1796]

[By BURNS; from *The Merry Muses of Caledonia* (*c.* 1800); tune, *Clout the Cauldron*].

You Jovial boys who love the joys,
The blessfu' joys of lovers;
An' dare avow't wi' daintless brow,
Whate'er the lass discovers;
I pray draw near, and you shall hear,
An' welcome in a *frater,*
I've lately been on quarantine,
A proven Fornicator.

Before the congregation wide,
I past the muster fairly;
My handsome Betsey by my side,
We gat our ditty rarely.
My downcast eye, by chance did spy,
What made my mouth to water,
Those limbs sae clean, where I between
Commenced Fornicator.

Wi' ruefu' face and signs o' grace,
I paid the buttock hire;

The night was dark, and thro' the park
I cou'dna but convoy her;
A parting kiss, what cou'd I less,
My vows began to scatter;
Sweet Betsey fell, fal lal de ral!
I am a Fornicator.

But, by the sun an' moon I swear,
An' I'll fulfil ilk hair o't,
That while I own a single crown,
She's welcome to a share o't;
My rogish boy, his mother's joy,
An' darling of his pater,
I for his sake the name will take,
A harden'd Fornicator.

THE BOWER OF BLISS

[*b.* 1796]

[An old Scots countryside song: from *The Merry Muses of Caledonia* (*c.* 1800), collected by BURNS (last stanza only by BURNS); tune, *Logan Water*].

Whilst others to thy bosom rise
  And paint the glories of thine eyes;
Or bid thy lips and cheeks disclose
  The unfading bloom of Eden's rose;
Less obvious charms my song inspire,
  Which fell, not fear we most admire,
Less obvious charms, not less divine,
  I sing that lovely bower of thine.

Rich gem! worth India's wealth alone,
  How much pursued, how little known;
Tho' rough its face, tho' dim its hue,
  It soils the lustre of Peru.
The vet'ran such a prize to gain,
  Might all the toils of war sustain;
A devotee forsake his shrine
  To venerate that bower of thine.

When the stung heart feels keen desire,
  And through each vein pours liquid fire;
When with flush'd cheeks and burning eyes,
  Thy lover to thy bosom flies;
Believe, dear maid, believe my vow,
  By Venus' self, I swear, 'tis true,
More bright the higher beauties shine,
  Illum'd by that strange bower of thine.

What thought sublime, what lofty strains
  Its wondrous virtues can explain?
No place, howe'er remote, can be
  From its intense attraction free.
Tho' more elastic far than steel,
  Its force ten thousand needles feel;
Pleas'd their high temper to resign
  In that magnetic bower of thine.

Irriguous vale, embrown'd with shades,
  Which no intrinsic storm pervades!
Soft clime, where native summer glows,
  And nectar's living current flows!
Not Tempe's vale, renoun'd of yore,
  Of charms could boast such endless store;
More than Elysian sweets combine
  To grace that smiling bower of thine?

O may no rash invader stain
  Love's warm, sequestered virgin fane!

For me alone let gentle fate
  Reserve the dear august retreat!
Along its banks when shall I stray?
  Its beauteous landscape when survey?
How long in fruitless anguish pine
  Nor view unveil'd that bower of thine?

O! let my tender trembling hand
  The awful gate of life expand!
With all its wonders feast my sight—
  Dear prelude to immense delight!
Till plung'd in liquid joy profound,
  The dark unfathom'd deep I sound;
All panting on thy breast recline,
  And, murmuring, bless that bower of thine.

THE TROGGER

[*b.* 1796]

[By BURNS; from *The Merry Muses of Caledonia* (*c.* 1800); tune, *Gilliecrankie*].

As I cam down by Annan side,
  Intending for the border,
Amang the Scroggie banks and braes,
  Wha met I but a trogger.
He laid me down upon my back,
  I thought he was but jokin',
Till he was in me to the hilts,
  O the deevil tak sic troggin'!

What could I say, what could I dae,
  I bann'd and sair misca'd him,
But whiltie-whaltie gae'd his arse,
  The mair that I forbade him.
He stelled his foot against a stane,
  And doubl'd ilka stroke in,
Till I gaed daft amang his hands,
  O the deevil tak sic troggin'!

Then up we raise, and took the road,
  And in by Ecclefechan,

Where the brandy-stoop we gart it clink,
  And the strang-beer ream the quech in.
Bedown the bents o' Bonslaw braes,
  We took the partin' yokin';
But I've claw'd a fairy cunt synsine,
  O the deevil tak sic troggin'!

SHE'S HOY'D ME OUT O' LAUDERDALE

[*b.* 1796]

[An old Scots countryside song; from *The Merry Muses of Caledonia* (*c.* 1800), collected and revised by BURNS].

There liv'd a lady in Lauderdale,
She lo'ed a fiddler fine;
She lo'ed him in her chamber,
She held him in her mind;
She made his bed at her bed-stock,
She said he was her brither;
But she's hoy'd him out o' Lauderdale,
His fiddle and a' thegither.

First when I cam to Lauderdale,
I had a fiddle gude,
My sounding-pin stood the aik
That grows in Lauder-wood;
But now my sounding-pin's gaen down,
And tint the foot forever;
She's hoy'd me out o' Lauderdale,
My fiddle and a' thegither.

First when I came to Lauderdale,
Your Ladyship can declare,

I play'd a bow, a noble bow,
As e'er was strung wi' hair:
But, dow'na do's come o'er me now,
And your Ladyship winna consider;
She's hoy'd me out o' Lauderdale,
My fiddle and a' thegither.

YE HAE LIEN WRANG, LASSIE

[*b.* 1796]

[An old Scots countryside song; from *The Merry Muses of Caledonia* (*c.* 1800), collected by BURNS; tune, *Up an' waur them a', Willie*].

Your rosy cheeks are turn'd sae wan,
Ye're greener than the grass, lassie,
Your coatie's shorter by a span,
Yet deil an inch the less, lassie.
Ye hae lien wrang, lassie,
Ye've lien a' wrang;
Ye've lien in some unco bed,
And wi' some unco man.

Ye've lost the pounie o'er the dyke,
And he's been in the corn, lassie;
For ay the brose ye sup at e'en,
Ye bock them or the morn, lassie.
Ye hae lien wrang, lassie, &c.

Fu' lightly lap ye o'er the knowe,
And thro' the wood ye sang, lassie
But hurryin' o'er the foggie byke,
I fear ye've got a stang, lassie.
Ye hae lien wrang, lassie, &c.

MUIRLAND MEG

[*b.* 1796]

[An old Scots countryside song; from *The Merry Muses of Caledonia* (*c.* 1800), collected and revised by BURNS; tune, *Eppy Macnab;* or, *The Campbells are coming*].

Amang our young lassies there's Muirlan' Meg,
She'll beg or she work, and she'll play or she beg;
At thretteen, her maidenhead flew to the gate,
And the door of her cage stands open yet,
And for a sheep-cloot she'll do't, she'll do't,
And for a sheep-cloot she'll do't.
And for a toop-horn, she'll do't to the morn,
And merrily turn and do't and do't.

Her kittle black een they wad thirl ye through,
Her rose-bud lips cry kiss me just now;
The curls and links o' her bonny black hair,
Wad put you in mind, that the lassie has mair.
And for a sheep-cloot she'll do't, &c.

An armfu' o' love is her bosom sae plump;
A span o' delight is her middle sae jimp;

A taper white leg, and a thumpin' thie,
And a fiddle near by, can ye play a wee?
And for a sheep-cloot she'll do't, &c.

Love's her delight, and kissing's her treasure,
She'll stick at nae price, an' ye gie her good measure;
As lang's a sheep-fit an' as girt's a goose egg,
O that's the measure o' Muirlan' Meg.
And for a sheep-cloot she'll do't, &c.

NINE INCH WILL PLEASE A LADY

[*b.* 1796]

[By BURNS; from *The Merry Muses of Caledonia* (*c.* 1800); tune, *The Quaker's wife*].

"Come rede me, dame; come tell me, dame,
"My dame, come tell me truly,
"What length o' graith, when weel ca'd home,
"Will sair a woman duly?"
The carlin clew her wanton tail,
Her wanton tail sae ready;
"I learn'd a sang in Annandale—
"Nine inch will please a lady.

"But for a contrie cunt like mine,
"In sooth we're nae sae gentle;
"We'll tak two thumb-bread to the nine,
"And that's a sonsie pintle.
"O leeze me on my Charlie-lad!
"I'll ne'er forget my Charlie!
"Twa roarin' handfu' and a daud,
"He nidg'd it in fu' rarely.

"But weary fa' the laithern doup,
"And may it ne'er ken thrivin';

"It's no the length that gars me loup,
"But it's the double drivin'.
"Come nidge me, Tam; come nidge me, Tam;
"Come nidge me o'er the nyvle;
"Come louse, aud lug your batterin' ram,
"And thrash him at my gyvel."

HOW CAN I KEEP MY MAIDENHEAD?

[*b.* 1796]

[From *The Merry Muses of Caledonia* (*c.* 1800); tune, *The Birks o' Abergeldie*].

How can I keep my maidenhead,
  My maidenhead, my maidenhead,
How can I keep my maidenhead,
  Amang sae mony men, O?

The Captain bad a guinea for't,
  A guinea for't, a guinea for't;
The Captain bad a guinea for't,
  The Colonel he bad ten, O.

But I'll do as my minnie did,
  My minnie did, my minnie did;
But I'll do as my minnie did,
  For siller I'll hae nane, O.

I'll gie it to a bonie lad,
  A bonie lad, a bonie lad;
I'll gie it to a bonie lad,
  For just as gude again, O.

An auld moulie maidenhead
  A maidenhead, a maidenhead;
An auld moulie maidenhead
  The weary wark I ken, O.

The stretchin' o't, the strivin' o't,
  The borin' o't, the rivin' o't;
And ay the double drivin' o't,
  The farther ye gang ben, O.

HERE'S HIS HEALTH IN WATER

[*c.* 1796]

[By BURNS; from *The Merry Muses of Caledonia* (*c.* 1800)].

Altho' my back be at the wa',
  An' tho' he be the fau'tor;
Altho' my back be at the wa',
  I'll drink his health in water.
I wae gae by his wanton sides,
  Sae brawlie's he cou'd flatter;
I for his sake am slighted sair,
  An' dree the kintra clatter;
But let them say whate'er they like,
  Yet here's his health in water.

He followed me baith out and in,
  Thro' a' the nooks o' Killie;
He followed me baith out an' in,
  Wi' a stiff stanin' p——
But when he gat atween my legs,
  We made an unco' splatter;
An' haith, I trow, I soupled it,
  Tho' bauldly he did blatter;
But now my back is at the wa',
  Yet here's his health in water.

JOHNIE SCOTT

[*b.* 1796]

[From *The Merry Muses of Caledonia* (*c.* 1800); tune, *O the broom*].

Whare will we get a coat to Johnie Scott,
  Amang us maidens a'?
Whare will we get a coat to Johnie Scott,
  To mak the laddie braw?

There's your cunt hair, and there's my cunt hair,
  Ar' we will twine it wondrous sma';
An' if waft be scarce, we'll cowe our arse,
  To mak him kilt an' a'.

DUNCAN GREY

[*b.* 1796]

[An old Scots countryside song; from *The Merry Muses of Caledonia* (*c.* 1800), collected by BURNS].

Can ye play me Duncan Grey?
  Ha, ha, the girdin' o't;
O'er the hills an' far awa,
  Ha, ha, ha, the girdin' o't.
Duncan came our Meg to woo,
Meg was nice an' wadna do,
But like an ether puff'd an' blew
  At offer o' the girdin' o't.

Duncan he cam here again
  Ha, ha, the girdin' o't;
A' was out, an' Meg her lane,
  Ha, ha, ha, the girdin' o't.
He kiss'd her butt, he kiss'd her ben,
He bang'd a thing against her wame;
But, troth, I now forget its name;
  But, I trow, she gat the girdin' o't.

She took him to the cellar then,
  Ha, ha, the girdin' o't;
To see gif he cou'd do't again,
  Ha, ha, ha, the girdin' o't.
He kiss'd her ance, he kissed her twice,
An' by-an'-bye he kissed her thrice,
Till deil a mair the thing wad rise,
  To gie her the long girdin' o't.

But Duncan took her to his wife,
  Ha, ha, the girdin' o't;
To be the comfort o' his life,
  Ha, ha, ha, the girdin' o't.
An' now she scaulds baith night an' day,
Except when Duncan's at the play,
An' that's as seldom as he may,
  He's weary o' the girdin' o't.

TWEEDMOUTH TOWN

[*b.* 1796]

[An old Scots countryside song; from *The Merry Muses of Caledonia* (*c.* 1800), collected by BURNS].

Near Tweedmouth town there liv'd three maids,
Who used to tope good ale;
An' there likewise liv'd three wives,
Who sometimes wagg'd their tail.
They often met to tope an' chat,
And tell odd tales of men;
Crying, When shall we meet again, an' again?
Crying, When shall we meet again?

Not far from these liv'd three widows,
With complexions wan an' pale,
Who seldom us'd to tope an' bouse,
An' seldom wagg'd their tail.
They sigh'd, they pin'd, they griev'd, they whin'd,
An' often did complain,
Shall we, quo' they, ne'er sport or play?
Nor wag our tails again an' again?

Nine northern lads, with their Scots plads,
By the Union, British call'd,

All nine-inch men, to a bousing came,
  Wi' their brawny backs an' tald.
They all agreed to cross the Tweed,
  An' ease them of their pain;
They laid them all down,
  An' they fuck'd them all round,
An' cross'd the Tweed again, an' again.

THE LASSIE GATH'RIN' NITS

[*b.* 1796]

[An old Scots countryside song; from *The Merry Muses of Caledonia* (*c.* 1800), collected by BURNS; tune, *O the broom*].

There was a lass, and a bonie lass,
  A gath'rin' nits did gang;
She pu'd them heigh, she pu'd them laigh,
  She pu'd them whare they hang.

Till tir'd at length, she laid her down,
  An' sleept the wood amang;
Whan by there cam three lusty lads,
  Three lusty lads an' strang.

The first did kiss her rosy lips,
  He thought it was nae wrang;
The second lous'd her bodice fair,
  Fac'd up with London whang.

An' what the third did to the lass,
  I'se no' pat in this sang;
But the lassie wauken'd in a fright,
  An' says, "I hae sleepit lang."

THE LINKIN' LADDIE

[*b.* 1796]

[An old Scots countryside song; from *The Merry Muses of Caledonia* (*c.* 1800), collected by BURNS; tune, *Push about the jorum*].

Waes me that e'er I made your bed!
  Waes me that e'er I saw ye!
For now I've lost my maidenhead,
  An' I ken na how they ca' ye.

My name's weel kend in my ain countrie,
  They ca' me the linkin' laddie;
An' ye had na been as willing as I,
  Shame fa' them wad e'er hae bade ye.

TAIL TODLE

[*b.* 1796]

[By BURNS; from *The Merry Muses of Caledonia* (*c.* 1800); tune, *Chevalier's Muster-roll*].

Our gudewife held o'er to Fife,
For to buy a coal-riddle;
Lang or she came back again,
Tammie gart my tail todle.
Tail todle, tail todle,
Tammie gart my tail todle;
At my arse wi' diddle dodle,
Tammie gart my tail todle.

When I'm dead, I'm out o' date;
When I'm sick, I'm fu' o' trouble;
When I'm weel, I step about
An' Tammie gars my tail toddle.
Tail todle, tail todle, &c.

Jenny Jack she gae a plack,
Helen Wallace gae a boddle,
Quo' the bride, "It's o'er little
"For to mend a broken doddle."
Tail todle, tail todle, &c.

O GIN I HAD HER

[*b.* 1796]

[An old Scots countryside song; from *The Merry Muses of Caledonia* (*c.* 1800), collected by BURNS; tune, *Saw ye na my Peggy?*].

O gin I had her
Yea, gin I had her,
O gin I had her,
  Black altho' she be.
I wad lay her bale,
I'd gar her spew her kail,
She ne'er soud keep a meal,
  Till she dandl'd it on her knee.

She says I am light
To manage matters right,
That I've nae might, or weight,
  To fill a lassie's e'e;
But wad she tak a yokin',
I wad put a cock in;
A quarter o't to flocken,
  I wad frankly gie.

HAD I THE WYTE SHE BADE ME

[*b.* 1796]

[An old Scots countryside song; from *The Merry Muses of Caledonia* (*c.* 1800), collected and retouched by BURNS; tune, ***Highland hills***].

Had I the wyte, had I the wyte,
  Had I the wyte she bade me?
For she was steward in the house,
  And I was fit-man laddie;
And when I wadna do't again,
  A silly cow she ca'd me;
She straik'd my head, and clapt my cheeks,
  And lous'd my breeks and bade me.

Could I for shame, could I for shame,
  Could I for shame denied her?
Or in the bed was I to blame,
  She bade me lie beside her?
I pat six inches in her wame,
  A quarter wadna fly'd her;
For aye the mair I ca'd it hame,
  Her ports they grew the wider.

My tartan plaid, when it was dark,
  Could I refuse to share it?
She lifted up her holland-sark
  And bade we fin' the gair o't;
Or how could I amang the garse
  But gie her hilt and hair o't?
She clasp'd her houghs about my arse
  And aye she glower'd for mair o't.

JENNY MACRAW

[*b.* 1796]

[An old Scots countryside song; from *The Merry Muses of Caledonia* (*c.* 1800), collected by BURNS; tune, *The bonny moor-hen*].

Jenny Macraw was a bird o' the game,
An' mony a shot had been lows'd at her wame;
Be't a lang bearing arrow, or the sharp-rattlin' hail,
Still, whirr! she flew off wi' the shot in her tail.

Jenny Macraw to the mountains she's gaen,
Their Leagues and their Covenants a' she has taen;
"My head now, and heart now," quo' she, "are at rest,
"An' for my poor cunt, let the deil do his best."

Jenny Macraw on a midsummer morn,
She cut off her cunt, and she hang't on a thorn;
There she loot it hing for a year and a day,
But, oh! how look'd her arse when her cunt was away.

OUR GUDEWIFE'S SAE MODEST

[*b.* 1796]

[An old Scots countryside song; from *The Merry Muses of Caledonia* (*c.* 1800), collected by BURNS; tune, *John Anderson, my jo*].

Our gudewife's sae modest,
When she is set at meat,
A laverock's leg, or a tittling's wing,
Is mair than she can eat:
But, when she's in her bed at e'en,
Between me and the wa';
She is a glutton deevil
She swallows cods and a'.

SAME TUNE

[BURNS]

My auntie Jean held to the shore,
As Ailsa boats cam back;
And she has coft a feather-bed
For twenty and a plack;
And in it she wan fifty mark,
Before a towmond sped;
O! what a noble bargain
Was auntie Jeanie's bed!

O GAT YE ME WI' NAETHING

[*b.* 1796]

[By Burns; from *The Merry Muses of Caledonia* (*c.* 1800); tune, *Jacky Latin*].

Gat ye me, O gat ye me,
  An' gat ye me wi' naething,
A rock, a reel, a spinning wheel,
  A gude black cunt was ae thing.
A tocher fine, o'er muckle far,
  When sic a scullion gat it;
Indeed, o'er muckle far gudewife,
  For that was ay the fau't o't.

But haud your tongue now, Luckie Lang,
  O haud your tongue and jander,
I held the gate till you I met,
  Syne I began to wander;
I tint my whistle an' my sang,
  I tint my peace an' pleasure,
But your green grave now, Lucky Lang,
  Wad airt me to my treasure.

WE'RE A' GAUN SOUTHIE, O

[*b.* 1796]

[An old Scots countryside song; from *The Merry Muses of Caledonia* (*c.* 1800), collected by BURNS; tune, *The merry lads of Ayr*].

Callum cam to Campbell's court,
  An' saw ye e'er the make o't;
Pay'd twenty shillings for a thing,
  An' never got a straik o't.
    We're a' gaun southie, O,
      We're a' gaun there
    An' we're a' gaun to Mauchline Fair,
      To sell our pickle hair.

Pay'd twenty shillings for a quine,
  Her name was Kirsty Lauchlan;
But Callum took her by the cunt,
  Before the laird o' Mauchline.
      We're a' gaun southie, O, &c.

Callum cam to Kirsty's door,
  Says, "Kirsty are ye sleepin'?"
"No sae soun' as ye wad trow,
  "Ye'se get the thing ye're seekin'."
      We're a' gaun southie, O, &c.

Callum had a peck o' meal,
  Says, "Kirsty, will ye draik it?"
She whippit off her wee white-coat
  An' birkit at it nakit.
    We're a' gaun southie, O, &c.

"Bonie lassie, braw lassie,
  "Will ye hae a sodger?"
Then she took up her duddie sark,
  An' he shot in his roger.
    We're a' gaun southie, O, &c.

Kind kimmer Kirsty
  I loe wi' a' my heart, O,
An' when there's ony pricks gaun,
  She'll ay get a part, O.
    We're a' gaun southie, O, &c.

JOCKEY WAS A BONNY LAD

[*b.* 1796]

[An old Scots countryside song; from *The Merry Muses of Caledonia* (*c.* 1800), collected by BURNS; tune, *John Roy Stewart's strathspey*].

My Jockey is a bonny lad,
A dainty lad, a merry lad,
A neat sweet pretty little lad,
An' just the lad for me.
For when we o'er the meadows stray,
He's ay sae lively, ay sae gay,
An' aft right canty does he say
There's nane he loes like me.
An' he's ay huggin', ay dawtin',
Ay clappin', ay pressin',
Ay squeezin', ay kissin',
An' winna let me be.

I met my lad the ither day,
Friskin' thro' a field o' hay,
Says he, "Dear Jenny, will ye stay
"An' crack awhile wi' me?"
"Na, Jockey lad, I darena stay,
"My mither she'd miss me away,
"Syne she'll flyte an' scauld a' day,

"An' play the deil wi' me."
But Jockey still continued
Huggin', dawtin', clappin', squeezin', &c.

"Hoot! Jockey, see my hair is down,
"An' look, you've torn a' my gown,
"An' how will I gae thro' the town?
"Dear laddie, tell to me."
He never minded what I said,
But wi' my neck an' bosom play'd;
Tho' I entreated, begg'd an' pray'd
Him no to touzle me.
But Jockey still continued
Huggin', dawtin', clappin', squeezin',
An' ay kissin', kissin', kissin',
Till down cam we.

As breathless an' fatigued I lay
In his arms among the hay,
My blood fast thro' my veins did play
As he lay huggin' me;
I thought my breath would never last,
For Jockey danc'd sae devilish fast;
But what cam o'e, I trow, at last,
There's deil ane kens but me.
But soon he wearied of his dance,
O' a' his jumpin' an' his prance,
An' confess'd without romance,
He was fain to let me be.

THE DOCTOR'S OUTWITTED

[*b.* 1800]

[From *Ane Pleasant Garden* (*c.* 1800); edited by C. KIRKPATRICK SHARPE].

Two able Physicians as e'er prescribed physic,
On Burlington's illness, were sent for to Chiswick,
Both took my Lord's pulse, and most solemnly felt it,
Then call'd for his urine, view'd, tasted, and smelt it.
On sight of the water, cries Mead, "It is plain
That my Lord has a fever, and must breathe a vein."
"You are right, Brother Mead, and besides," added Sloan,
"Who voided this water, had doubtless a stone."
"You are out," quoth the nurse, "you both of you miss'd it,
For it was not my Lord, but my Lady who piss'd it."

CALD KAILL OF ABERDENE

[*b.* 1800]

[From *Ane Pleasant Garden* (*c.* 1800); edited by C. KIRKPATRICK SHARPE].

The cald Kaill of Aberdene
  Is warming at Strathbogie;
I fear 'twill tine the heat eer seen,
  And neer fill up the bogie.
The lasses about Bogingicht,
Their leems they are baith cleer and right,
And if they are but girded right,
They'll dance the reell of Bogie.

Now, Aberdene, fat did ye mean,
  Sae young a lass to woo man,
Im seer to her it is nae mows,
  Fat e'er it be to you, man.
But women now, are nae sae blate,
But they ken auld folks out of date,
And better playthings they can get
  Than castocks in Strathbogie.

THE WEE ONE

[*b.* 1800]

[From *Ane Pleasant Garden* (*c.* 1800); edited by C. KIRKPATRICK SHARPE].

A slee one, a slee one,
 I neere saw sic a slee one;
The first night that I with him lay,
 Oh, then he gott this wee one.

This wee one, this wee one,
 This bonny winking wee one;
I'de bin a maide amongst the rest
 Wer't not I gott this wee one.

GREEN BROOMS AND YELLOW

[*b.* 1800]

[From *Ane Pleasant Garden* (*c.* 1800); edited by C. KIRKPATRICK SHARPE].

Green brooms and yellow,
  Green brooms and yellow,
She was a minikin lass,
  And he was a —— dronsie fellow.
This minikin lass and this —— dronsie fellow
  Went out to weed the rigges,
And fain he would have f—d her,
  But he could not unbutton his breeks.
Green brooms and yellow,
  Green brooms and yellow,
She was a minikin lass,
  And he was a —— dronsie fellow.

This minikin lass and this —— dronsie fellow
  Went out to reap the oats,
And fain he would have f—d her,
  But would not lift up her coats.
Green brooms and yellow,
  Green brooms and yellow,
She was a minikin lass,
  And he was a —— dronsie fellow.

DRUNCK AND SOBER

[*b.* 1800]

[From *Ane Pleasant Garden* (*c.* 1800); edited by C. KIRKPATRICK SHARPE].

Drunck and sober again,
  Drunck and sober again,
But I shall ne'er be merry at heart,
  Till I'm drunck and sober again.
I took her about the middle,
  And laid her upon the grass,
And the wind it blew up her cloaths,
  That you might have seen her arse.
Drunck and sober again,
  Drunck and sober again,
But I shall ne'er be merry at heart,
  Till I'm drunck and sober again.

TOO COLD TO LY ALONE

[*b.* 1800]

[From *Ane Pleasant Garden* (*c.* 1800); edited by C. KIRKPATRICK SHARPE].

Dearest Jeany, thou must love me,
  Troth, my bonny lad, I do;
Since thou sayes so, come I'll prove thee,
  Dearest thou must kiss me too.
Take a kiss or two, my own dear Jockie,
  For more I dare give none, I trow;
Fush, quoth he, be not unlucky,
  Pray, wedd me first and all will do.

Not for all Fife and lands about it,
  I'll ne'er wedd for to be bound,
Neither can I live without thee
  For fyve hundered thousand pound.
Then thou will dy if I forsake thee,
  Better dy as be undone;
Since thou sayes so, come I'll take thee,
  It's too cold to ly alone.

www.ingramcontent.com/pod-product-compliance
Lightning Source LLC
Chambersburg PA
CBHW021044030726
47496CB00006B/1684
9783744777957